Saving Ivy

Safe and Secure, Book 3
Alyssa Bailey

I0671424

Saving Ivy

Safe and Secure, Volume 3

Alyssa Bailey

Published by Alyssa Bailey, 2021.

This is a work of fiction. Similarities to real people, places, or events are entirely coincidental.

SAVING IVY

First edition. February 12, 2021.

Saving Ivy Description

First, she stole his heart and left him bleeding. Then she stole from the Mob. Now he is the only one who can save her. Will his price be too steep for Ivy to pay?

Kaden was perfect for super-rich, too spoiled Ivy Linton. When Kaden rescued Ivy and then took her home, it was soon obvious to all that they were falling in love. Soon, however, the realities of the dangerous nature of his job frightened her. Her own crazy life was already scary enough, so Ivy left one evening without a word. She struggled to overcome the nightmares, the loneliness, and the loss of the only man she had ever loved. Now, a year later, the old worries were gone, but new troubles have emerged. Her mother is married to a mob boss, his second in command wants her, and she witnessed him commit murder. So, what should she do? Steal important information for life insurance and run like hell to the only safe person she knows.

Ivy was surrounded by trouble, but that's what he was trained to deal with in the military and now with Reynaud and Associates, of which he was one. So when Ivy left without a word a year ago, he was crushed but let her go expecting her to return. She didn't, until now. Amid the chaos of a bombing, his girl shows up full of secrets and the Mob on her tail, but she can still rock his world with a look. He was too gentle the first time. Now he must take control if he is going to keep her safe. And this time, he would make sure she stayed.

***Saving Ivy is the 3rd book in the Safe and Secure Series. It can be read as a stand-alone, but it's recommended you read the books in order for maximum enjoyment. Saving Ivy has a backstory that can be read in the final book of the O'Connor Series, Forever Molly.

Love the inside scoop? Sign up for my newsletter with special offers, bonus content, and more.

https://www.alyssabaileyromance.com[1]

This book is a work of fiction. Names, characters, places, and incidents are products of the author's imagination or used fictitiously. Any resemblance to actual events or locales or persons, living or dead is entirely coincidental.

Copyright © 2021 by Alyssa Bailey

Cover Design by Pro_ebookcovers
Edited by Marybeth Renn
Manufactured in the United States.

Acknowledgments

Now is the time for thanking the incredible people who helped me get this story to you:

Marybeth R. Thank you for taking my work and putting that final, intimate polish on my words to make them glow.

To my Betas: Thank you for your on-point suggestions and wonderful insight. You enhanced Kaden and Ivy's story.

To my ARC team: Thank you for reading, reviewing, sharing and helping this work be seen. You are the best!

To my husband: You are the love of my life. Thank you for giving me that first encouragement to step out and find new places to share my passions and for always supporting me through the angst.

Prologue

The air was thick with the smell of dying embers and the feeling of disbelief. The cement dust had settled, but the air was thick with emotion. The elite group of operatives at Reynaud and Associates joined the other observers as they stared at the partially devastated building. Their faces held various expressions of horror, dismay, and critical analysis. All they had ever known as a cohesive team in the civilian world centered on these leased offices on the edge of downtown Lexington. It looked like a modified version of an all too familiar war zone, the likes of which this group was entirely too familiar.

Consequently, Jac's talk of relocating due to inadequate security safeguards would happen now. Kaden Trainer moved in closer to get a better look. An assortment of quiet voices murmured as the head of the much sought-after security company stood contemplatively silent. Jacquard Reynaud, retired military officer and civilian operative, began to assess the situation with almost clinical detachment, a skill he had honed well in his many years of commanding top military forces. A gift his people at Reynaud & Associates had all come to appreciate.

Knowing the non-operative employees would be wondering what they would do now, likely concerned for their jobs, Kaden knew without a doubt that Jac had already begun to plan their next move. It was also well-known that Jac often tried to keep his cyber demon wife, Sharlee, at home with Storm, their one-year-old son. Unfortunately, since she was the person who discovered the intel that the building was a target, his logical, protective reasoning was overridden. Kaden smiled to himself. Jac must have known it was a useless waste of his time to attempt to thwart his master web-crawler wife's decision to join them here, especially when they employed a very capable nanny.

Besides, Sharlee didn't follow directions well unless she wanted to. She never had and probably never would. That was one of the reasons Kaden and Sharlee were best friends. He kept her out of trouble, and she kept him entertained… usually. He was the only male operative on his team who hadn't wanted to slap her butt for something stupid. No, since he met Ivy Linton after she had been kidnapped and then found in Montana, Kaden had only wanted to keep one woman out of the line of fire and in his arms. Unfortunately, she hadn't been as committed to him as he was to her.

Earlier today, Sharlee had discovered that their office building was the target for a mob hit. As soon as she'd followed the trail to verify that it was directed by La Cosa Nostra, the deed had been done. It wasn't Jac's team's fault, this time. It wasn't *his* slow intel that had landed them literally on the street, business-wise. The relief of non-culpability was so strong, he almost laughed, but the building he was looking at inspired anything other than humor.

Charlotte, the name only her husband used these days, snuggled into the protective hold of her husband's embrace, and experienced an overwhelming sense of sadness. This was where she had first met Jac, where they had first worked as a team, and where she had been called Sharlee for the first time. It was where she had first figured out what FUBAR and some of the more colorful uses of NATO's phonetic alphabet meant.

It was in this building that she had fallen in love with not only the men running ops as a team and the job she had been offered but the man who orchestrated everything. She'd fought in this building and made love in this building. She'd stared down evil and even done a little matchmaking. And now, it was gone. Oh, it might be repaired, but her husband would never allow the team to operate from here again. Once it had been compromised, it was all over. The search would begin for another location, and he would look for higher or lower ground, whatever he thought would keep them all safe.

Kaden stared at the rubble and tried not to flashback to his last military mission but trying to avoid getting sucked into his past sometimes took super-human strength that he didn't always possess. His mind drifted back to that day. He was reminded of the stench in the air of burnt soldiers and villagers. He could see the small and large fires, some completely out of control, surrounding the area he and his team occupied. He could hear the yelling and the nerve jarring screams of frightened, injured civilians as they filled his ears. Kaden could feel himself slipping closer to the mental precipice.

Luckily, he wasn't drawn into the horrific Venezuelan town scene this time, but the events were playing on a loop in his mind's eye as he surveyed the similar scene before him today. On that day, the little cluster of huts on the outskirts of Caracas had exploded without warning. Exactly like this building had. Only this wasn't a war-ravaged country; it was Lexington, Kentucky. In Venezuela, there were no invaders they could see, no enemy to retaliate against, just the huge hole that was left in the place his buddies had been. Here, they could root out the culprits and find justice.

On that last mission, when the rubble had stabilized enough for Kaden to pull himself out of the wreckage, only two had survived. He, with a messed-up elbow, and Fanelli, the newest team member, stood to the side without a mark on him. Unlike that experience in Venezuela, this time, the outcome was better. Few were in this structure when it exploded. And to the best of their knowledge, no one had died, but it was early yet. The guard's office was on the other side of the bottom floor, so it was possible that the explosive device had been left in a corner and detonated before it had been detected, just like in Venezuela.

Involuntarily, Kaden's mind drifted back to the final moments before that explosion and his later suspicions as to what had really happened in that little village and who was responsible. He didn't want to suspect his teammate, but Fanelli didn't just survive; he was literally unscathed. Kaden still wondered about the circumstances that had taken Fanelli from that hut at precisely the right time and for no apparent reason. They were due to be extracted the next morning, and all was quiet.

The villagers were happy to have been protected from the latest pillaging attack, which coincided with the end of his team's successful mission. Kaden had been the last one to grab some grub and take a leak. He was also the one who saw his teammate leave quietly as though he were slipping away. Fanelli said that he was going to retrieve something from his pack, but afterward, Kaden had always wondered. Why was Fanelli in such a great hurry?

Kaden had been just outside the strike zone, on his way inside to eat when it happened, so his injuries were minimal. He sustained a crushed elbow because a piece of equipment flew into him. Kaden counted himself lucky, and it took him a long while to deal with the loss of four incredible soldiers and two handfuls of civilians. Fanelli had feigned surprise at the explosion, but his performance hadn't been credible.

Even today, Kaden quelled the urge to look around for Fanelli. Of course, he wasn't here. But someone had to be responsible for this. Just like in that South American village, someone had to have blown up the Lexington office building. Unfortunately for them, there was no evidence to direct them where to look for answers. If Sharlee hadn't intercepted a cryptic message and deciphered it quickly, they wouldn't have been able to make the call to evacuate, which saved the few who were in the building at the time.

Some of the businesses that had office space there might have drawn unwanted attention, but they were closed today as well. Only a skeleton maintenance crew and the security team were working. This event was planned and executed to make a statement, not to kill large numbers of people. That was the difference. The military team was the target in Venezuela, but not here.

"Trainer." a far-off voice broke through his reverie, followed by someone shaking him. "Kaden, is that Ivy?"

Ivy, the woman he wanted and couldn't have. He forced his thoughts to back away from the horrific memory and its mystery. It was a dangerously slippery slope if he followed too far down that rabbit hole. This was his family now. Kaden looked around him. In his heart, the men of his military team would always be his brothers in arms, but Jac's team also stood beside him through whatever shit storm rained down on him. His first team was gone, but Jac's was here now, and Kaden was grateful that he had found them.

Garrett, perceptive as always, leaned in close. "You good?"

Kaden relaxed his shoulders. "Yeah, thanks."

"I recognize that glazed, faraway look. Shake it off and go talk to your girl. She is definitely one to find trouble if it lingers too long."

Kaden wanted to contradict him, but Ivy Linton had already proven Garrett right several times.

"I hope she isn't part of this shit," continued Garrett.

Kaden watched for a minute, and his co-worker was right. She seemed hesitant to approach and yet, desperate to do so. "I don't know what's going on here," Garrett swung his arm to encompass the damaged building. "Or with you two, but I don't think this is the last we've heard of the group who did this."

Kaden grunted his agreement. Sharlee thought she might find out, but no one was attaching responsibility or blame to anyone until they verified their intel and did more digging. They needed to find out who was behind this shit and, more importantly, who was their target. It would take a while.

"Go see your girl. We'll have time to figure things out later."

"Trouble crawls out of the woodwork when she is around, she never goes looking for it, but her choices... that is another matter."

"I hope you're right." Garrett leaned away to look at Ivy. "That girl is connected to the equestrian kingpins, the country club set, and probably the governor. After the racehorse caper with her crazy relatives that took you to Montana, her people are just high enough to think they can get away with anything. If it were me, I'd send her cute ass far in the other direction."

Kaden inhaled deeply then released. "Damn. She can rock my world by just standing there all cute and shit, but you're right, this isn't the place for her. I thought I knew her, but I never did, not really."

"I'll let you tell her that, okay? A determined woman is more up your alley than mine, Trainer."

Kaden nodded. He did have a way with words, and Monroe called him the Whisperer when Sharlee was in an uproar over things. Kaden had settled Ivy a few times too, but she said she needed some time. He'd respected her decision even if he didn't agree. Kaden tried to be sensitive to Ivy after the kidnapping. He had held her hand after the Feds scared her into testifying for her freedom. Later, when Ivy had learned her freedom was never in question, he'd foolishly let her go without trying to figure out a better solution and regretted it.

He hadn't regretted much in his life, but Venezuela and Ivy were the two that had changed the way he looked at life. And this security company had saved him both times. This might be his chance to change the course of their lives, or he might be fucking it up more. But if there was a chance, he wouldn't waste the opportunity. He'd be the man she needed, not the one she thought she wanted. He looked up at Ivy, still standing hopeful of his attention, and he hoped she could handle it.

IVY STOOD OFF TO THE side, longing to step into Kaden's sheltering arms but afraid of rejection. She'd left him thirteen months ago to figure her life out after the fiasco that played out near that large Irish family, the O'Connors in Montana. She'd forced herself not to call him. To give them both some breathing space to work things out. It hadn't turned out to be what they'd needed, what she'd needed. She'd hated every moment of it.

This morning, she had decided she couldn't do without Kaden any longer. Her life had not improved, it had actually gotten worse, and the only thing she had gotten a handle on was the realization that she had to try to get him back. Deciding to take a chance was hard enough, but to come to his office only to find this unholy scene had shaken her more than she'd realized.

Her hands were shaking, and she felt cold inside. Fear that Kaden might have been working in the building when the explosion happened made her sick inside. On the way to Kaden's office, the news report had said a building just off the downtown area, but she hadn't known the name of Reynaud and Associates' building until she arrived.

Ivy fingered her pendant as she frantically looked for the man she'd voluntarily walked away from. If she couldn't locate Kaden, maybe one of his co-workers was in the crowd. She saw Carter, that gentle behemoth of a man standing at the corner of the spectators, so she headed for him. Kaden came into view as he stood next to Sharlee. The rest were there as well, but Ivy only had eyes for Kaden. She steered her steps toward him.

He'd seen her but didn't make a move at first. It was like he was looking past her or through her. Ivy hesitated. Maybe this wasn't such a good idea. Her legs slowed their forward motion and then stopped. A man, Monroe, or Garrett, she couldn't remember which, leaned down to speak with Kaden. There was another man she didn't recognize who stepped over to speak to Carter.

Several ladies she hadn't really gotten to do more than meet last summer were there as well. *Turn away forever or stay and deal with the consequences*, she told herself. The dilemma was causing chaos to reign supreme in her brain, and Ivy didn't know what to do, but she knew what her heart wanted, and it was now or never.

Then Kaden was walking in her direction. Oh no, that wasn't a smile of welcome on his face. His face was serious, and he looked like he was going to send her away. *Brave front*, Ivy told herself. She knew this might happen. Risking rejection in the hopes of acceptance seemed worth it at the time, but now? She couldn't face him. Couldn't do this. She turned to leave before he made it to her.

"Ivy, stop."

That wasn't a request. Damn her body. When Kaden spoke in that tone, she not only couldn't ignore his direction, but she also couldn't stop the tidal wave of tingling emotions that overtook her. She stopped.

Ivy began to mentally coach herself. *You can do this. Smile. Offer condolences for the building and those caught inside. Then, if he doesn't want you to stay, turn and go.* Saving face was important if her heart was about to be broken. She had been disillusioned before, but Kaden had never been anything but honest with her. She had to admit that this man could annihilate her with his rejection. Her stomach churned.

"Ivy, leaving again so soon?" He was not happy to see her.

"I-I was worried." She pointed to the building. "I heard on the radio."

"It took an explosion to bring you around? What would it have taken a year ago to keep you here?"

"Kaden, I was chaos walking. I had to get my life figured out."

She didn't know where she found the strength to be chastising with this man who could control even her breath if she let him. He was always kind and gentle with her and courteous to others, but when things became serious and dangerous, she had seen him break a man's jaw with little effort.

"Hey, you're right. I'm sorry. Been a rough day so far but seeing you makes it better." His voice was gentle and caressing like a spring breeze. Kaden's face morphed to concern. It was hard to return his gaze as he studied her. "Sweetheart, what are you doing here?"

Sweetheart. Good. That was so good. "Um, I was on my way to see you when I heard this building had been bombed. Are you hurt?" She stood back to look at him as if she were assessing a property.

"Nope, we took the three-day weekend off for Veteran's Day, but there were some people still in the building, I guess. Injuries I hear, but no casualties. It wasn't a big bomb."

Turning back to view the scene again, "That's amazing."

"It is. Now, tell me why you were coming to see me?"

He crossed his arms and took a step back, ready to listen before judging. That was Kaden Trainer. His tone said he was in charge again, and Ivy embraced the systemic response and clenched with the ache. Ivy was tired and felt rudderless. She needed someone to take the helm for a while. She needed Kaden to steer.

Her family was messed up with no remedy in sight. Her dancing clinics were just getting off the ground before this whole underworld chapter of her life began. Being kidnapped, then leaving Kaden, and becoming tangled up in her mother's way of life had been exhausting. The Feds had taken their pound of flesh and then left her alive but bleeding.

Now, she didn't have any place to offer her clinics, use her psychology degree, or do her Indie graphics. She didn't even have a place to lay her head without fear of discovery. FUBAR, she had heard Jac call a similar situation: Fucked up beyond all repair. That summed it up pretty nicely.

Since her kidnapping by a guy she had just met and that whole adventure in Montana with Molly O'Connor's family, life had changed. Ivy kept in contact with the O'Connors, but yesterday, while she was chatting with Molly, that insightful woman told Ivy to go and get what she wanted. There was no reason to live without the man of her dreams.

"These men, once hurt, do not go after what they want without incentive. Kaden wanted you badly. He'd fallen for you. We all commented on it later. Now, I get that you needed a little break, but sulking and licking your wounds is over. I promise you there will be some making up to do and some hard conversations to be had, but it will all be worth it in the end. I'm speaking from experience, Ivy. Call him or just show up. You have to tell him that you need him, that you feel lost and unable to navigate the world without him, and that's all it will take. I promise."

Well, she'd taken Molly at her word. The woman lived with a family full of Kaden-type men. She must have some idea about the workings of their minds.

"I missed you and needed to see you. Wanted..." Ivy suddenly looked horrified. "Girlfriend. Oh, Kaden, do you have a girlfriend? I'm so sorry. Is one of those women, I mean, is she here?"

Kaden shook his head as he pulled Ivy into his arms. "Hush, sweetheart. I don't have a girlfriend. Why would I when I was waiting for you to figure out you belong right here in my arms?"

"Really?" She had to see his face. "You haven't moved on? You still want me? After I left for so long?"

"Oh, I still want you, but do you want me? You chose to leave without talking. And you need to realize the rules governing my life haven't changed. My expectations are what they were when you met me and when you walked away from me."

"But not because we weren't good together. I left to find out how I really felt about my whole life. Rules?" but she could feel her face heating up. "I'm not sure I remember any rules."

"Ivy, you know there are things important in my life. I live by certain rules, and you did too. I'll refresh your memory later. For now, are you coming back to stay, play, or just passing through?"

"That isn't what I did, Kaden. I wasn't just playing around. I needed the space."

"From us?"

"From everything. I stayed for months at the lake house my father left me. I had to make sure the feelings I had for you weren't tied up with that whole ordeal."

"And were they?"

"Yes, some of them, but my deeper feelings were independent of that mess. I-I also felt unease about the type of work you do. I wondered about the risks you take, the amount of danger. I had to decide if it was an acceptable level for me."

"I'm glad you understood when you needed to take a step back to think about those things, but I expected better. We *deserved* better. There should have been a real conversation, not a bolt to the nearest exit."

"I know. I'm sorry I didn't know how to tell you. I couldn't explain my feelings because I didn't understand them myself. I panicked."

Kaden nodded. "Why didn't you come back after you decided we were good."

"I had the trial over that kidnapping and the horse theft to wait for, and by the time they had a plea bargain, it had been nine months. I worried it was too long."

"Then why did you change your mind now?" Kaden was not making it easy for her, and for a second time, she wondered if she should just leave. Her recent experiences made her stay. Kaden was the only one who could or would help her out of the mess she found herself in.

"Counseling and Molly O'Connor. She said I'd regret it if my feelings were still strong and I didn't try to put things back together. I decided she was right."

"If I take you back now, you have to agree to my way of handling things."

"Kaden, I can take care of myself. A relationship with you doesn't mean I'm giving up my autonomy."

He smiled and hugged her tight again. "Good, because I don't want a clingy woman in my life, but when I say something is for your safety or health, you will have to trust me."

"You mean if I don't see the health or safety hazard myself."

"I mean, if I say there is a problem, you believe me."

"Of course. When have I not listened?"

"Montana? And right here, last year, when I said I knew there was a problem and going home wasn't safe nor advisable. Sharlee offered her home, you accepted then disappeared. We tracked you until you got back to your mother's place, but do you know what that did to me?"

Ivy shook her head. "Not then, but as I figured things out in my mind, I realized what happened. I was scared." She hoped her expression showed how she'd beg for his forgiveness if necessary.

Kaden brushed Ivy's wind tousled hair away from her face. She ached at the seriousness of the man she knew she loved. "When you're confused or have questions, you aren't going to run off and hide; you will come talk to me." Not a question.

"Yes."

"And I'm the boss when one is needed."

"Oh, but... Um, okay. That's acceptable."

Kaden cocked his head to the side and openly scrutinized Ivy. "You don't sound sure."

"I am. It's just a big step. I like to be my own boss, but I miss you so much it hurts. I want to agree with your way of doing things, but I'm afraid I don't know how to let go. What if I can't?"

"Ivy, do you want to be with me?"

Ivy's shoulder muscles, held tight, seemed to tighten even more. "Isn't that what I've been saying? But what if I can't be all you want?"

"I know you can because you were before you left."

"I was? Then I guess I'm here to stay if you'll have me."

"Is that a formal commitment? Because I want you, but I've already gone through the pain of losing you once. I won't do it again." He pulled back to stare into Ivy's face.

"I suppose I am if there is an "us.""

"Oh, there's an "us" sweetheart. It has taken you a while to work it out, but there has always been an us. You've just been on a long hiatus but no more, understand? I need you in my life every day, not just when it's convenient. If you stay, there is no leaving. We will move heaven and earth to make this relationship work. I'm in for the long haul. If you stay, so are you."

The fearful uncertainty vanished in the wake of Ivy's growing annoyance. "I told you. I didn't leave you because it was convenient. Nothing in my life has been convenient in the last year and a half. Don't be such an ass."

Kaden threw his head back and laughed without restraint. "I have missed you, honey."

The irritation melted away in a smile. "I've missed you, too."

"Okay then." Kaden kissed the top of her head.

"Okay, then what?"

His head swooped closer and warm kisses tickled Ivy's lips. Gentle pressure gave way to a deeper, probing kiss, his tongue showing a slight impatience to enter her warmth. Before his libido and control were gone, his head was lifting.

"Okay, then stay. And Ivy? You're due one whopper of a spanking for leaving me hanging for so long."

Kaden delivered a tight squeeze and a touch of his lips on her temple before ushering her toward the group he'd just left. These people were intelligent, accomplished, and self-assured.

They intimidated her. Perusing the gathering now, as she reluctantly drew closer, nothing had changed.

A man, Monroe, she thought, was speaking to Jac, who nodded. "We need to reorganize and figure out what our next move is. See you bright and early tomorrow morning, my place." There were murmurings and short conversations. A woman that Ivy remembered as Becky, Jac's office assistant, spoke up.

"I sent an email to the support team and to the other agents, um, employees. Told them it won't be but for a few days and to enjoy these days off with pay."

"Jac, with pay?" asked Jessie. Ivy understood the question. Jessie was the accountant and with another co-worker, Mark Jensen.

Jac grinned. "You heard me right. Sorry. I know that you're doing your job and looking out for the company's solvency, but you'll just have to keep good records and add them to our insurance claim. You and Becky can figure it out. But for now, Charlotte needs to get back home to Storm and her computer. We need to figure out what triggered this event and make sure we can track those fuc...he caught Charlotte's eye, "er... fox-trotters down.

The group began to disperse amid chuckles as they headed to their respective vehicles. Each greeted Ivy as they passed her as though she'd never left the inner circle. It was disarming and oddly comforting as though she had been accepted back into their select membership. It was a ridiculous thought, for they had to be wary of her after her unexpected exodus.

Ivy was always both off-kilter and fascinated by Kaden's friends. Just as she began to understand one aspect of the group, a new layer of complexity showed itself. If she were wearing her psychology hat, she would have been fascinated with her reactions to them and their dynamics. Now, however, she was simply exhausted.

Their women knew how to deal with things, and Ivy could follow their lead. She was a fast learner. She resolved to ask questions and pick their collective brains for anything she needed. She would be comfortable with them if it killed her because they were Kaden's second family, and he was her only trustworthy friend.

Kaden's hand slid back into its familiar place at the small of her back as he bent down. "You can follow me home. Not a good idea to leave your car in this area right now. Is anyone expecting you tonight?"

Ivy sighed. "Not for well over a year now. Have you moved?"

"Nope."

"Then I won't tell you not to drive too wildly because if I lose sight of you, I know how to get to your place."

Kaden grinned. "I remember you enjoying driving fast with me, but I promise I'll behave tonight."

"I hope not all night," said Ivy, risking a saucy look in his direction.

"I'll follow your lead, sweetheart."

A warm rush raced along her veins as she indulged her imagination and envisioned what a night of passion could look like after a year apart. Kaden had already been her knight in shining armor in Montana, and he had been with her through the interviews with all kinds of alphabet agencies until they were sure she was innocent of any crime.

That didn't stop them from trying to force her to testify. Kaden was everything Ivy had needed at that time and more, but her insecurities had hijacked her good sense. She left him for the familiar on her family's horse ranch except, there was no security in that place. Not anymore. When the reality of her mistake had hit home, Ivy had decided to talk to Kaden, but life events stopped her.

Finally, after waiting for months to cross the bridge of past errors and admit she was lost without him, here she was. Ivy knew what devastating loss meant, but she had gotten used to being tossed out to sea without a paddle or a life jacket. She was born into money, but Kaden had lived a charmed life. It seemed he still did. It sounded as though Jac had the resources to take them somewhere else quickly. And Sharlee was amazing at doing the impossible on the computer.

No, Kaden would be fine. But would she? This could put a wrench in her plan to re-establish her relationship with Kaden. He'd kept his hands to himself, played the gentleman, except for that kiss and a guiding hand on her back. Ivy hoped that would end in his condo. She had craved his touch, his words that told her he was in control. She needed his mastery of her body, mind, and inner self. She'd been spiraling out of control these last months.

Ivy had barely escaped prosecution because many people believed she was part of the horse thefts, but Thorne, the federal officer in charge of the case she had been dragged into, had spoken up for her. She went on to spill her guts to the prosecution and escaped being charged for a crime she hadn't known was in progress.

It was after that when her world really got out of control. Ivy shook off the memories of the last few months, all her horrible choices and risky behaviors culminating in her mother pushing her into the wrong man's path. Kaden still wanted her, and she wanted him. That would be enough for now. Hopefully, it would be enough to overcome the roadblocks.

Chapter One

Kaden watched as Ivy Linton weaved her way through traffic on her way to his condo. He had decided that the best way to keep her safe and in his sight was to follow her. She said she remembered where he lived, so he gave her the lead in case her memory was faulty. It wasn't. They pulled up into his garage, and she allowed him to go ahead of her as she had done many times before. He spoke to the parking attendant, gave her I.D., a copy was made, and a picture of her plates taken. It made her nervous that someone had information on her. It never did before, but things were different now. Hugely different.

"I'll take the temporary pass for now, but she will need a permanent one. She's staying permanently. Who do I talk to for that?" They parked, then Kaden placed the pass on Ivy's rearview window. He led her to the elevator.

"Permanently, Kaden?"

"Yep. We can talk about it once we are in the condo."

There was no small talk on the way to his condominium. The silence was thick as they entered the large, two-bedroom home on the fifth floor. Kaden turned off the alarm from his phone before entering, and once inside, he reset it knowing Ivy was watching him warily.

"You came to me, Ivy. This is safety, not captivity. Anytime you want to leave, you can, but I hope you won't. At least not until we have had some time to clear the air and build on what we started last year. Any leaving now will be mutually agreeable."

"That's fair. I'm just cautious now."

Kaden nodded but didn't answer. She should wonder what would happen next, after taking off and leaving without a word of warning. At least Ivy knows she's earned a punishment for how she handled things last year. Until Sharlee had found her that night, he'd worried that she was in danger. She hadn't even taken all of her clothes and things. He was out of his mind with fear that she had been kidnapped again by people from the same group who had taken her before. He'd eventually packed her things and put them in the spare bedroom. He couldn't bear to get rid of anything.

To her credit, Ivy had called him a week after she left to say she just needed some time to herself. Kaden had tried to be sensitive to her thinking. He'd told her he understood, but in reality, he didn't. He had concluded that it highlighted the lack of trust she had in him and he had in her. To be totally honest with himself, he now acknowledged he'd been over-protective from the start. He had smothered her with his care because of her ordeal. Kaden had thought she'd need a few days, but those morphed into a few weeks. Soon they became months that had ultimately been thirteen months.

Ivy was showing her fear. She sucked on her lip, ultimately biting it lightly. A tell that she was nervous, worried about something. Then she rubbed her hands. "Maybe this wasn't a good idea. Maybe too much time has passed."

"It was a good idea, but you need to understand that I'm going to be more careful due to our past." He watched her squirm. Definitely something was going on.

"Then why say I would need a permanent pass? You aren't making sense."

"It's what I want. I want us to work, and I'm going with that mindset. I'll fight like hell to make this work, but I'm going to ask some hard questions in the next few days, and I'll expect nothing but honesty. I will create the best environment for the best result, but in the end, it will be up to you."

"I expected that."

"Did you?" He was dubious. "I may be more cautious, Ivy, but I still crave you. I've not dated since you left."

Her look of surprise told him she had. Kaden hadn't realized how much that gutted him, but he'd let her speak. It had been his choice, after all.

"I've tried a couple of times, but they never progressed past the first date because no one compared to you. Not a spark. Not even a little twinge. You've ruined me for anyone else."

Kaden couldn't help the grin that spread across his face. "That works for me. Oh, and you need to know that Sharlee will have to look into your last year. She'll need to make sure nothing has gone on that would compromise the company or us. It would make things difficult if there were, but I think we're good there."

"I haven't done anything worth investigating." Was that apprehension?

"Great, then it will come up clean. Sharlee will have to review the court tapes concerning you, but that should just be a formality, right?" He watched her reaction.

"Of course." Kaden raised his eyebrow in question. "If you have something you need to share, now would be the time, Ivy. If I know what I'm going to hear tomorrow from Sharlee, it will make my explanation smooth."

Kaden listened as Ivy glossed over his insinuation as she played with the pendant always around her neck. "I promise I did not engage in any illegal acts if that's your question. I might have spent some time with people I later learned were unsavory, but I separated from their company."

"Like whom?"

"You know, people that hung around my mother and my uncle. He had debts, and my mother paid them off, but she had little time for me except to introduce me to some of her associates." Ivy shrugged. "Suave, but creepy, you know? After a few times hanging out, I stepped away. It got a little messy because they wanted to keep me in their circle, but I figured if I stayed away from my mother and her friends, they would forget about me. It must have worked because I haven't seen or heard from them in a while."

Kaden handed Ivy a glass of her favorite wine and chose not to call her out on her deceit, but she had several tells. As Ivy looked away to the left, he watched her display her most used tell when she was hiding something. Rather than say anything, Kaden concentrated on his glass of wine, but he took a mental note of the story her body was telling him. He'd held onto the bottles he had in his cabinet waiting for her return, and when she hadn't, he'd forgotten about them. Tonight, he was glad he had. Taking her soft, warm hand in his cooler one, Kaden led Ivy to the sofa.

He returned to the conversation. "Such as who? I need a name, Ivy." Her restless unease did not escape him, but he made no mention of it.

"I don't know their last names. One they called Bubba and said we were in Bubba Land whenever we went to his gaming place."

"Gaming place? Was that the name?"

"No, just a joke. I think Bubba owned the gaming den where lots of people would come by and play for hours. Some stayed for the whole day until closing. Kingdom Games, that's what it was called. Someone said it was a play on words, but I never got the joke."

Kaden fixed his gaze on her as he thought about the implications of that name. Either scenario that he arrived at was not good, and it surprised him how his gut clenched in aggravation. She had been in a place that was obviously a safety issue. More than once by the sounds of it. This time he didn't mind that he showed his displeasure. Ivy looked away.

"Bet he made a lot of money." Could she have been looking for someone in her economic class?"

Ivy shrugged. "Probably." Truthful, good.

"How about the others?"

"Others? I don't know. I mean, I didn't know most of them, and usually, they didn't say their names. I got the impression I shouldn't ask. JJ was the one I hung out with most days. There was someone called Senior, but he didn't talk to me, and I was glad. He had a Doberman Pinscher face, and I bet he was just as vicious." Ivy shivered as she recalled the man.

Kaden spoke his tone heavy with censorship. "So, you dated—"

"No, I *hung out* with JJ. We *never* dated. He often dropped by the gaming room, and I would end up leaving because they got caught up in something or other, and he would tell me to go home. I did because I wasn't interested in what they were doing. After a few weeks, it became obvious that my first impressions were right. JJ was nice enough, but he forgot about me easily. I could have murdered someone, and he wouldn't have known. Not like..." she stopped talking, but Kaden knew what she had been about to say. "Why are you grilling me?"

Kaden ignored the last question. "He didn't pay attention to you like I did."

"Yes." The air was still. "Look, maybe this wasn't such a good idea. I'm not ready for this. Being with you is... intense."

Kaden reached over and touched her cheek, sliding his fingers down her smooth skin. "Yes, you are, sweetheart. You've taken the first, hardest step. The rest will be easier."

"Promises, promises."

Her attempt at being jovial fell flat when the desperation in her eyes met his searching ones. He nodded an unvoiced decision and stood with determination.

"I'm going to feed you, spank you, and then bed you. Do you have any objections?"

His eyebrow quirked, daring her to disagree. Heat pooled in Ivy's eyes, and he imagined her core was feeling the tension as well. Watching her squirm reminded him of when she would rub her legs together to relieve the tingle. Her lips tipped up on one side.

"We can skip dinner and the rest," her voice seductively hopeful.

Kaden laughed. "I think you've been skipping too many dinners lately, woman, and I intend you don't skip too many more. And the spanking is something you need. We both do." He grabbed her hand and pulled her close. "I'll ravage you soon enough. You owe me a helluva lot of makeup."

He took her lips with his, falling into the kiss, drawing sweet nectar from them. As the caress deepened, Kaden drew back with a moan of reluctance. Ivy released a sigh as her answering protest.

"Soon, baby. First things first."

Kaden whipped up a pasta and vegetable dish quickly as he worked hard at making Ivy relax with anecdotes of the team. He plated their meal while Ivy filled their glasses again. They chatted like old friends as they ate dinner. The ease of their reconnection warmed him. He wasn't wrong about them belonging together. Enjoying Ivy's beauty and her sassy sense of humor woke his latent libido and heated his desires.

When Kaden stood to put their plates in the sink, he was suddenly hit with a hyper-alertness accompanied by an overwhelming sense of danger. Something was wrong. Instinctively, he shifted his attention to Ivy, a protective move he had done many times in their early relationship. His gut clenched in fear, the hairs on his neck tingled. He never ignored his gut.

Like so many soldiers and operatives throughout history who had developed their sense of safety based on the way their inner workings directed. Kaden knew something was very wrong. His gut was cramping, and his inner calm began to morph into steel-encased coldness, preparing to do what was necessary for survival.

He listened as he kept his attention on Ivy. She wasn't doing anything but growing curious, likely wondering what she had done wrong. Her expression was one of confusion, changing to unease.

"Kaden?"

He tried to rationalize with himself. There was no reason to be on guard in his own home, yet the feeling could not be overlooked. Just as Kaden opened his mouth to warn Ivy to get her things, the phone rang.

He spoke as he simultaneously grabbed his handgun from the kitchen drawer. "Get your things, quickly, Ivy. We need to go."

He listened as the person on the other end of the line began rattling off instructions in a terse tone. "Trainer, incoming. Take your alternate route. Someone will meet you at the rendezvous."

"Roger that."

The phone was pocketed, his coat on, and his second gun holstered by the time Ivy had picked up her own coat. Looking down to check Ivy's shoe choice for the day, Kaden nodded approval at her sneakers.

"I'll explain later, but remember when I said you have to listen to me when I say it's for your safety?" She nodded, wide-eyed. "This is one of those times, baby."

She sucked in a breath. "But..."

Grabbing the coat from her, Kaden pushed Ivy toward the back of his condominium, her protest lost in the urgency of his manner and movements.

"Where is your phone?" he'd asked.

"My pocket."

He looped his arm through the strap of her purse on the sofa and brought it with him as he guided her toward the very back bedroom closet.

"My purse." She tried to turn back, but Kaden didn't allow it.

"Got it."

Shoving her through the walk-in closet door, he closed it behind them. Kaden felt Ivy watch as he removed a remote from a shoebox on the closet shelf. He punched a button, and the back wall swung around 180 degrees, opening to a small compartment, similar to those hidden rooms in old spy movies.

Kaden walked Ivy onto the dais that appeared and hit his remote again. It was a tight squeeze, but he needed to stick with his girl. He knew something wasn't right, and now this was the proof that things were very wrong. It was going to get tricky.

IVY REMEMBERED THE last time she was this scared and hated the way she'd panicked. Bubba and JJ were nothing to shake a stick at, and Ivy hadn't told Kaden the whole truth. She hadn't been able to leave JJ as easily as she'd implied nor as long ago. In fact, Ivy had told JJ she was coming over last night and simply had not gone home. She tried to shake off the worry that he had something to do with Kaden's building. No, that was ridiculous.

After leaving her house as casually as she could, she had stopped to buy some clothes because she didn't want it to look suspicious when she drove away from the house on the family property. She'd come straight to her only place of assured safety. Had they followed her to Lexington, to Kaden's condo? Even if they followed to the building, they couldn't get past the parking attendant. How would JJ know which condo was Kaden's even if they came in the front door?

She was immediately pushed out of the hidden door that had opened to the other side of the wall. It was dark as pitch. Overwhelming fear clutched her heart. Darkness had not been her friend in recent years, and she wasn't about to repeat any of those horrible events. Nothing good happened in the dark.

"Hold on, baby," he whispered. "I'm grabbing a flashlight."

The light was minimal, but it seemed to illuminate everything and nothing at the same time. Kaden's strong, warm arms were suddenly wrapped around her and his soothing voice caressing her ear as he whispered into it.

"Shush, baby. I know this is frightening, but we're fine. I need you to stay quiet while I get us to the rendezvous and safely to Jac's house. We'll figure things out there. Yeah?"

Ivy nodded, and Kaden's lips left a soundless kiss before he moved away, taking his comfort and warmth with him. Her hands wrapped around his arm tightly as Kaden silently led them through the darkness to a door that seemed to appear out of nowhere. They exited, crept down a covered stairway, and through another metal door into the night, which seemed almost glaringly bright after the near absence of light they had come from.

Kaden was immediately on alert once they emerged into the dirty alleyway. Watching him as he scanned the area quickly but thoroughly reminded Ivy how fast she had fallen for Kaden, her hero, when he had protected her from all comers after her rescue. Then he had stood against reporters, waited while she had endless meetings with law enforcement and attorneys, and soothed her fragile nerves when she was overwhelmed.

Ivy followed Kaden closely and clung to him while watching a car inch its way up to the alley entrance. She shivered with cold and apprehension as a flashlight shined its light in what appeared to be code. Kaden pulled her to the vehicle.

What if it was a trap? Ivy could feel herself begin to pull back. Kaden didn't slow his approach, scooping her into his arms tighter, bringing them both closer. When they reached the large SUV, he practically threw her into the backseat, throwing her back to the moment she knew she was being kidnapped. She tried to rationalize through the rising panic. Just when her breath seemed to leave her, and her terror had overcome her, Kaden crammed in behind her. The door was still closing as the car drove off at what seemed like great speed.

After a few moments when Kaden and Monroe talked in stilted abbreviated syllables, Kaden leaned back and pulled her toward him. "You good, Ivy?" Kaden spoke to her so quietly, she had to concentrate on hearing his voice.

"Think so." He pulled her closer. She exhaled. Her heart pounded less now, no longer loud in her ears. No longer violently trying to escape from her chest any longer. The residual effects, however, were still felt. Ivy thought she was done with panic attacks, but this was too close for comfort.

"Do I get to use my rubber paddle?"

"Sorry, man, not today."

"Damn. I haven't had a good butt to warm since Sharlee, and I still didn't get to use my paddle. And territorial. You are all too touchy about your women. Shit, at this rate, I'm going to have to find my own beauty to get my thrills."

"Shut up, asshole. Ivy's spooked enough already."

Monroe responded with apologetic compassion. "Sorry, Ivy. I'm teasing... mostly. I don't know what makes you so popular these days, but you sure are. You're in the right place here with Kaden and us, though. We'll figure this out. No one messes with us, and you are ours."

Ivy sat up and leaned forward. "Ours? But I don't understand."

"It's a good thing, Ivy, promise. Kaden will explain later, but you are definitely ours. I imagine you have been for the last eighteen months or so. Ever since Kaden here found you in Montana, drawing all kinds of attention from the Feds. You've just been too risky trying to do things alone. I think we are looking at the results of that loner life. Kaden will fix that, too. We're headed for Jac's place, so sit back and enjoy the ride. It won't be long now."

Ivy leaned into Kaden's beckoning arms and laid her head on his chest. The deep rumble she heard and felt infused her being with a comforting calm she hadn't really felt since she walked away from him last year. A difficult but necessary move. She hadn't appreciated him until she didn't have him and then didn't know what to do to get him back. Well, not without compromising her pride. But that was all over. She was here, and he wanted her. Now to keep it that way.

After her run-in with Bubba's group and JJ not wanting to let her go once she had hung around him for a short while, she was scared. Obviously, they were up to no good and possibly into things that were very... very bad. She knew that returning to JJ would have put paid to her personal freedoms forever, and eventually her life. Ivy didn't know why, exactly, except it was the vibe they had put off. And especially after what happened that last afternoon she was with him.

Kaden and his friends had an air about them too, but it was more like an immovable wall of protection if you were in the inner circle and an impenetrable barrier if you were outside them. She needed to be inside their perimeter. Ivy needed Kaden inside, outside and surrounding her.

He took care of her, commanded her compliance in a way that engendered a feeling of security. And inherent in that safe boundary were freedoms she had never experienced with another person before. The things she had discovered with him had her yearning for more.

Monroe was right; she was Kaden's, but did that mean the whole team became her protectors as well, like the O'Connors in Montana only with a twist? It was what Monroe had implied. That frightened Ivy as much as soothed her. Jac and his crew were a formidable force and one not to take lightly.

Ivy felt as though she were going from the frying pan into the fire, but she didn't fear she would be consumed. She somehow knew she would be refined by the experience. The process sounded painful and somehow right. She would be scorched if she had to reveal the whole truth. There should be no need for them to find out what she knew about JJ. She dozed for the rest of the drive until Kaden woke her.

"Hey, sweetheart. We're here." Ivy jerked awake.

"Whoa there, baby. We're at Jac and Sharlee's."

As Monroe slid his SUV into the spot open on the circle that sat in front of the house, Ivy tried to locate where the road was; however, she couldn't see it. The drive that led up to the grand entrance was long, totally obscuring them from any lights on the main road or the guard gate.

"Ivy, you stick with me and do as I say. I'm not sure what's going on, but we'll figure it out."

Kaden noticed that the number of cars matched the team members. It was at that moment that he knew something was up. Really up. Inhaling deeply and holding it for a count of five, he released the tension and changed his mindset. Someone was threatening their inner circle, and it was time to get serious. He wondered if it was connected to Ivy or the building, or both.

Jac owned a large spread, had a pricey stable full of quarter horses and standardbreds, and an immense, southern style country home. He'd inherited the property from his father when Reynaud senior decided to retire to Corpus Christi ten years ago. Jac then retired from the military. The stables he had grown over the years, and the house he'd refurbished slowly. The security was something he added once he started up the business and hadn't lessened it over the years. Good thing. They needed it now more than ever.

Jac met them at the door, stepping out of the way when Monroe kept walking. "Thanks, man."

Monroe replied cheerfully. "Yep. Didn't get to use my paddle, though."

Jac barked a laugh. "I wouldn't think so. You know our women are off-limits. I keep telling you to get your own." Monroe grunted and walked further into the house.

Kaden pulled Ivy closer and exchanged a loaded look with his boss before taking Ivy through the doorway. "Den?"

"Yep. Our new situation room for now."

"Should I settle Ivy first?"

"Nope. She's the key if I interpret this right."

Ivy spoke up. "What? I have no idea what you're talking about." Jac raised his left eyebrow.

Kaden rubbed his hand up and down Ivy's arm in reassurance and a little warning to not overreact. Kissing her cheek, he responded to Jac. "The visitors?"

"Looks like it. We'll figure things out, but I think you better stay out here for now. Your place is hot."

"Why?" asked Ivy. Her voice illuminated her question wasn't just curiosity but concern.

"Charlotte has put together what she knows about things so far, and we'll see what we need to do next. Tonight's events, along with the office building this morning, would seem to indicate that we have our plates full without trying to keep up with you. We don't want you wandering out in the world right now."

"It looks like the placement of the incendiary device was an inside job. The cameras were disconnected for eleven minutes at 5:30am this morning. Shift changes for security and when maintenance arrives. It opens suspicion for all three shifts, and that will take a little bit to work through. Normally, I like the challenge, but Charlotte says I can't get excited when one of our own's life is in danger. So, it will be much easier keeping you safe here, even if it isn't as much fun." Jac stopped and turned to look sternly at Kaden. "I am correct in assuming that is what we want to do, right Trainer?"

"You would be correct."

Jac nodded and turned back to continue toward the den. "Good. It always works better if Charlotte is right in her assessments."

Kaden laughed. "Roger that."

Chapter Two

Ivy walked into the Reynaud den and marveled that it was so well equipped. Obviously, this was meant to be a den, but Ivy imagined nothing was as it seemed with this lot. The deep wood on the floor under tasteful carpets with Native American motifs was enhanced by two walls of heavy built-in bookcases, and the remaining walls were dominated by two large desks.

One desk, with its two long additional desk lengths, was full of computers and electronics. The other held an assortment of typical office trays, a blotter pad, and other essentials of the owner of a highly sought-after securities company with both public and covert operations. The full extent of the jobs this company took on was not shared with non-essential personnel of which she was one. Ivy didn't care because after the whole ordeal with the horse stealing and her kidnapping from Kentucky to Montana, Ivy was happy not knowing.

"Charlotte hired some of Gray's team to relocate her office in here. When this is over, and we have a place to do business again, I'm reclaiming my den," said Jac, loud enough for his wife to hear him.

"Then get to work and make that happen," she answered him without looking up from her computer screens.

When she had felt overwhelmed by the trial prep and then the trial, she had begun to withdraw. Then, adding the emotional entanglement of her growing and then ending of the relationship with Kaden, Ivy had begun to feel she was drowning. Finally, walking away from Kaden and this way of life without a word had dried up communication lines between this group and her quickly.

She didn't expect any of these people to trust her, but in like fashion, she was still leery of them and their motives. They had not said much after Ivy appeared at their destroyed building without warning but were not unwelcoming. She reminded herself that it was encouraging.

Ivy knew she and Kaden had much more to talk about, feelings to work through, but the moment she had seen him, she had to hold herself back from running to him. She didn't doubt that Kaden was who he said he was, and anything he withheld from her was for her safety. These men were all about following the rules, their rules.

They, like her, were going to be careful with their secrets, and that was okay for now. In fact, if she was honest, the less knowledge of JJ's group and their activities that she was asked to disclose, the better for her.

Charlotte Reynaud finally looked up and over at the trio as they entered further into the room. "Hello, Ivy. Sorry about that 911 to Kaden, but it was the only way to keep you two safe. He was literally outgunned. If I remember correctly, you don't shoot, right?"

Ivy remembered Charlotte's assessing eye when she first met her over a year ago and again when she'd appeared earlier today. Now, after spending time doing what she did best, routing out the truth, the woman who could go into an internet wormhole and retrieve what she wanted now seemed less intense, less demanding.

Had Ivy passed her scrutiny? Or was it because Sharlee knew all there was to know? Ivy discounted that because it wasn't possible. The only one who had the whole story was Ivy, and she was beginning to believe she had only a small portion of the truth. Her head hurt, and she was beginning to become confused herself trying to figure out what this group already knew about her last year.

With a sigh, Ivy answered Sharlee's probing question. Always seeking more information, it was disconcerting that Jac's wife seemed satisfied with a mere negative response.

"It's all good, Sharlee. You would be correct. I don't shoot."

Kaden spoke firmly behind Ivy. "And I want it to stay that way."

"But she should be able to protect herself," protested Mark, who had forced Jessie to practice until her aim and delivery would keep her safe until help arrived. The intense member of the group, Garrett, nodded in agreement.

After glancing at Kaden, who smiled encouragement, she responded. "I have a 3rd-degree black belt in Taekwondo and a black belt in Karate. I had started teaching when all this happened. I know other crafts but do not practice them often."

Carter laughed out loud, and Monroe said, "Atta girl."

Garrett and Mark didn't seem impressed.

Sharlee's slow smile appeared. "That's awesome. Did you get that recently?"

"I had a black belt in Taekwondo but practiced hard to make it to the level I am now. I just got the black belt in Karate."

Charlotte made an excited little sound. "You and I are going to talk later."

Kaden intercepted Jac, who mumbled as he turned to head off to the coffee pot. Garrett was strangely quiet. She wanted to ask where Levi was, the other member of their team that Kaden had told her about over dinner, but honestly, she was too worried about things to care right now. Kaden returned with two bottles of water and sat her down on one end of the multi-sectioned sofa.

"Okay," said Monroe, "Let's get our plan of action settled on so we can go to bed. I figure we can't do much about the intruders until Sharlee finds out who they are."

Sharlee nodded. "Yes. I have two things right now. It appears as though the building was an inside job. I need to go through the video and account for everyone on their rosters and employee lists. Just because they are not on the CC TV doesn't mean they weren't scheduled, or they weren't there and then left. Besides, the missing video could have hidden any number of things and people."

Garrett spoke up. "Seems to me it is reasonable to assume the person who placed the bomb did not stay and work the next shift, making those on shift at the time of the explosion the less likely culprits."

"Yes, unless they were there and walked out on a break or something," said Kaden, drawing on his own suspicions of his previous experiences.

"Yes, that's true. We'll need to work out the scenarios. I've got the facial recognition running on the guys that came for a visit without calling first, but I think I know where they're from."

Garrett prodded her. "And?"

"Oddly enough, it's one of those Mafia-like gangs that have moved into the Lexington area these past few years. Horse thieving has picked up, as we all know. These mob extension families fix races, sabotage horses, grab women, kill men, and train teens to do as they want. I don't like it. They don't seem to be more than a little better than average, technologically speaking, so we can be thankful for that. However, what they don't know about in technology and the internet seems they are making up for in brute force and cunning plans. They have connections."

Carter uncrossed his leg and leaned forward to grab Ivy's attention. Becky wasn't with him, and it didn't look like Jessie had come either. They were protecting their women but from her or just the situation? She wanted to ask but didn't dare. Not yet. Carter spoke.

"You wouldn't know anything about these people, would you?"

"What kind of question is that, Carter?"

"The good kind. Look, Kaden, no offense, but Ivy is gone a year, shows up on Kaboom Day and then is with you when people get past the front entrance security and knows where to go? It doesn't sound good." Carter turned back to Ivy. "Ivy, I'm not saying you did this on purpose, but there is too much of a connection for it to be a coincidence."

"But I didn't know I was coming until last night."

"Oh? Why is that?"

"I hadn't tried to call Kaden yet. I know the timing looks bad, but I honestly don't know about any of this. I didn't even know the bombing they talked about on the radio was your building until I got there this morning."

Sharlee jumped in. "Okay, then why today?"

"I was talking to Molly O'Connor, and she encouraged me to call Kaden. I spoke to her two days ago. Call her and find out what she told me. I promise, it was something that just came up, and I thought it was now or never."

Kaden kept her in his arms as he spoke. "Ivy had hung out occasionally with a guy her mother introduced her to named JJ. She also met someone named Bubba. At least Bubba sounds like trouble. JJ is an associate of Bubba's."

"Would you know them if you saw them again?"

"Sure, but they wouldn't have been bothering Kaden. They don't know where I am."

"And you don't think anyone you know or have met would have come after you so aggressively?"

"Well, I don't know. Some of the guys at the gaming place were pretty rough looking. If I can get a picture, I might be able to identify someone, but they don't sound like anyone I've run across. Well, except last year, and you all know about that little adventure. Why do you ask? You don't think I had anything to do with whatever this is, do you?" Ivy knew why Carter asked. She had shown up at just the right moment. Maybe it was JJ's plan all along, to destroy the team's trust in her, to get her kicked out of the nest like a mama bird to a sick baby.

Ivy was beginning to sweat, and she took a nervous swig of her water. Kaden had leaned back and placed an arm around her shoulder, but he didn't stop anyone from asking their questions. She wondered what happened to her overprotective boyfriend.

"Some members of that community have been seen in and around your uncle right after he came home from prison last month," added Jac.

"Oh. I haven't seen my uncle since the day he went to jail. He isn't very social now, as you can imagine, and my aunt left him, so..." Ivy shrugged.

"I see," said Garrett. "But have you met the people your mother and her boyfriend hang out with?"

"You mean her new husband? Some. JJ was one of them that I met through Carlton."

Sharlee snapped her fingers. "Thanks, that helps me a lot. I bet I can cross-reference the photos to those at the wedding or reception." Sharlee turned back around and sat at her desk. The woman had six screens. Six.

Kaden spoke low. "It's a lot, I know, but she is in heaven when she has so many. I'm a two-screen man but, to each his or her own." Ivy nodded and added louder, "She didn't have a professional photographer. Her friend took them."

"Monika or Julia?"

"Monika. Um, how do you know that?"

"They call me Vapor for a reason. You figure it out."

Monroe stood again. "Okay, I'm tired, and if we could check on Levi, I'm good with keeping Ivy here until further notice. Does anyone expect you in the next few days, Ivy?"

"No, but is that really necessary?"

"Someone is after you," said Jac. "It's important that you stay low and out of sight until we neutralize the threat."

"By neutralizing, you mean what exactly?"

"Render the threat impotent," said Sharlee from her desk.

"Aw, baby. I tell you not to use that word with virile men around. It's just wrong."

Ivy started to laugh and tried to cover it in a cough. The others joined in with groans of pseudo injury. Garrett stood as well, followed by Carter.

"So, Sharlee is working on finding out who our after-dark visitors were, and Ivy is staying here until further notice. When are we coming back? Do we need to secure Kaden's place, or do one of us need to stay there tonight?"

Mark spoke up. "No, I had Levi lock it up and reset the alarm. They set the alarm off and ran. Sharlee remotely disengaged it, but we do need to pull and review Kaden's surveillance feed tomorrow. Too bad we don't own that camera, but we can wait."

"I'll tap into their system in the morning and copy it for us," said Sharlee casually.

"Charlotte, I told you we do things through the front door if we can," said Jac.

Sharlee made a face. "It takes so long that way. Besides, my way is fun."

"It's been too long, hasn't it?" asked Jac tenderly. Sharlee didn't answer, but she seemed to soften.

Carter said, "Right, I'm out. Becky isn't sleeping well, and this morning's rude awakening and tonight's call will have her up until I get home. Did you send a message to Levi?"

Jac nodded. "Yep, just sent him home as there have been no new sightings, and the members of that particular organization have left."

Sharlee added. "I suggested he secure and cover your car, Ivy. That okay with you?"

"Oh, he can't. I have the key here."

Kaden shrugged. "Levi doesn't need keys." His arm slipped around her waist. That action suddenly seemed controlling. Normally not her thing, but right now, Kaden in control felt good.

"He doesn't need... you know what, never mind." Ivy had hit her limit.

She grabbed her purse, suddenly overwhelmed with the events of the evening and the realization that she had been on the fringes of not just some aggressive men, they were connected to the mob. Now things made more sense, and she was definitely more scared.

"I go where Kaden goes. No offense, but he's my safe person."

"Good, because I'm staying too." Kaden stood as well and pulled her tightly to himself. "Now, did Levi leave no trace?"

Sharlee nodded, keeping her sight on the screens in front of her. "He'll get her car here sometime, but after they figure it's safe."

"Fine, and you keep it here until this mess is over. Any driving will be done by me and any errands I'll handle."

"Kaden..."

"Not up for discussion, Ivy."

The gruff, no-nonsense tone stopped any argument Ivy thought to have over his edict, although she suddenly wanted to slam into the sofa and cross her arms like an adolescent. *Real mature, Ivy*. It was what she had wanted, for Kaden to take over. He was. She took a deep breath and released.

"I still don't know how anyone knew I was here and parked in a garage or which condo I was in."

Jac stopped pacing. "Obviously, you were followed or, more precisely, tracked."

"But why?"

Jac continued. "My guess is that either you have something these people, whoever they are, want or know something they don't want, or *you* are someone they want. Or all of the above. We'll do a sweep. But until things are under our control, the only way to keep you safe is to stay here. When you think of a reason why they would want you, let us know."

"Who are 'they?'" asked Ivy.

"I'm working on that. I'll know tomorrow for sure," said Sharlee. "Yes, and that reminds me that you need Kaden to teach you about the Keep Safe program and then use it if needed. It could save your life."

"I don't even know who "they" are, so until I do, I'm not going to over-dramatize things." Her rapidly beating heart said otherwise.

Garrett seemed to think differently. "Oh, I'm pretty sure you know who these people are, and you likely know what they want, in part, anyway."

Maybe she did know something, but was it enough to go after her and now Kaden? Unlikely. There had to be more to the story than this, but for the life of her, she couldn't figure it out. Maybe her mom knew something. Surely it wasn't what she'd seen and later heard. No one knew she had still been in the building, except... no, he couldn't have heard it that far in the front of the building. She'd slipped out and left just as JJ had thought she'd done.

Sharlee's voice broke through Ivy's thoughts. "Oh, and I sent your mom a text message. You're going to the Martial Arts competitions in Memphis that starts next week. Your mom responded quickly and said, 'Good to know. JJ always goes first class. Enjoy.' She isn't worried about you, and that's good news for us. We have until a week from Sunday to figure this out. I hope we get it by then. But who is JJ? Will she run into your mom before then?" Sharlee turned from her screens to face Ivy, whose expression must have answered her question.

Sharlee spoke as realization dawned, and the room got quiet. "JJ isn't a woman."

Chapter Three

Ivy shook her head. "No, but before you come up with all kinds of scenarios, just let me say that he is an acquaintance, not even to the level of a friend. I went on a not quite date my mom set up and sat in the other room while JJ conversed for thirty minutes at least. I left before he came out. He asked me out again, I declined. Later, he was at some of the same gatherings I was, and he tended to stay close then disappear."

Garrett, who had taken his seat again, said, "Like he was conducting business at these gatherings."

"I never thought about it but, it could have been what he was doing. He's a friend of Carlton's and showed up at the house off and on. Whenever he tried to cozy up, I moved away. I kept my distance as much as possible. He offered to take me to pick up my car from the shop, my mother was conveniently unavailable, and I allowed that. On the way, he received a call and said he had to make a stop before getting me to the shop. After trying and failing to find him inside the building, I called an Uber."

"And?" prompted Jac.

Ivy shrugged. "And nothing. That last encounter was at the beginning of the week. That's the end of the story."

"How irritated was he that you left." Garrett seemed to have read between the lines very well.

Ivy shrugged again, but she felt anything but nonchalant. "Oddly, I guess he thought I would stay around. That's according to my mother, anyway. I'm not okay being treated like that by anyone."

"Was your mother put out with you or him?" asked Monroe, who had never gotten up from his seat.

"Both? I don't bother with her much anymore. She lives a different life than I do, except I live on the grounds in a manager cabin. I'm moving out as soon as I find a good place. I have money from my father before he died, and I teach martial arts privately, I do graphics for hire for fun, and I have a degree, so thankfully, I don't have those issues."

"What did your mother get?"

"From Dad? The horses and the property. He settled money on me and his lake house. I got it when I was twenty-five. Since I was past that when he died, there was no waiting period."

Mark turned to ask, "Why not live at the lake house?"

"I did for about six months, but I was starting to give private Taekwondo lessons, and it was too far from my clients. Besides, it's too cold during the winter."

"Why? You have a master's degree in psychology. Why would you teach martial arts?" asked Sharlee, "Or do graphic design?"

"Less stress, until now. I need a full Ph.D. to be able to actually do something with that degree. Look, I hadn't had it long before the mess last year. I was a psychological mess myself after that kidnapping and later events. I couldn't surround myself with others dealing with trauma while I was still dealing with my own. It's one of the first things you learn. I don't know if I'll finish the degree."

Garrett continued to probe. "How many people know about your inheritance?"

"My mom, the attorney, and now you all."

"And her husband?"

"Maybe. I don't know."

Sharlee spoke up. "Well, if her new husband knows, then I bet the mob knows. I see him with other known members of that Lexington gang. He just came up as a suspected known associate on the DEA's site. I don't know his connection yet, but it isn't looking good. And I'll bet that is why you are so interesting to John Jester, the man you know as JJ."

Garrett spoke. "Shit. Are we talking about Carlton Marciano? He's your mother's husband?"

"Yes."

"Damn, sugar, he's the head of a minor family. Not in full power, but definitely has power and is greedy as hell. He has his fingers in so many pies, he has run out of fingers. The DEA might say, "suspected," but they mean connected."

"What? No, you have to be mistaken." But looking at the screen, at his face, Ivy knew he wasn't, and neither was Sharlee.

"I just pulled him up. Man, the Feds have a huge dossier. He is bad business. Do you think your mom would listen if you told her about the mob connection?"

"I think she might know. She likes nice things, and she pretty much gets what she wants now, and Carlton is gone most of the time. She likes that too, although I think she genuinely does care about him."

Jac spoke up. "Charlotte's right. If that's your property on her screen and that is your net worth, the mob sees your mom and you as easy pickings."

Kaden spoke up. "Baby, they're right. Marciano married your mother with an agenda. You both have sweet properties and impressive assets. Yours is out of the way and big. That's a nice chunk of change in your bank accounts. Bringing you in and your resources would be a big prize for someone who wants to move up in the organization. It would definitely impress Marciano if they got both of you."

Mark said what no one else did. "Unfortunately, if you don't fall into step with their plans, your life is in real danger. If you die, who gets your assets?"

"My mom, I guess. I don't have a will."

Kaden completed the thought. "And her husband. Sharlee, we need to change that asap."

"But I thought it was... what should I do? I promise you I had no idea."

Jac nodded. "Go to bed. We'll work on this tomorrow. Charlotte, go to bed. Your son will soon be looking for a midnight snack. The rest of you, go or stay. But be back here tomorrow at 9 a.m., with Becky and Jessie."

The goodbyes were murmured as the other men left the house to their own homes. Ivy was exhausted, and Kaden naturally took over.

"We will be down for breakfast," Kaden assured them as he led Ivy from the room.

Kaden placed his hand at the small of her back to gently propel an exhausted Ivy up to the room he always used when at Jac's. He shut the door to the speculations Jac and Sharlee were tossing around as they prepared to go to bed. He wanted to relax Ivy and ease those tight shoulder muscles. A little massage and some playtime might do the trick, but he wasn't going to overstep the boundaries. They hadn't been together for over a year. Kaden had changed in some ways, and he knew Ivy had.

Early in their relationship, it had been difficult getting past the events at the O'Connor's ranch, but Molly O'Connor and Sharlee had helped so much. Even Jocelyn O'Connor had counseled Ivy virtually for several months to help Ivy move past the trauma. The dreams lessened, and by the time Ivy had decided she needed to take a break and regroup, waking up in a cold sweat was rare.

Because of her degree, she had analyzed the fear and the whole situation better, but it still took time for her subconscious mind to believe her conscious reassurances. When that finally happened, it coincided with the grand jury, and then there were the plea deals. She wasn't off the hook until each person charged had accepted and been sentenced. For her safety, it had been arranged that she would go to Jac and Sharlee's, where the security could easily be beefed up if she felt too vulnerable. One day, she went to court, came home while he was on the job, took most of her things, and left. He hadn't seen her again until today.

Kaden had feared she would never come back. In fact, he had decided that if she didn't return by the end of a year, he would start changing his thinking and put himself back in the dating game. He didn't want to even consider it when the time came, and today, Ivy had made it unnecessary.

But was she ready for a serious relationship? He hoped so because he was tired of chasing skirts and enduring long dinners with incompatible women. They were all nice in some ways, but no one clicked like he and Ivy. Going back on the market after loving Ivy would have been a nightmare. One he wasn't sure he would have ever been able to do. Ivy was it for him.

His cock wasn't even the first thing that told him she was the one for him. His protective instincts were on high alert. His heart melted whenever she teared up, unable to handle her sadness. Unless the tears were brought on by his doing because she'd gone too far. He could handle them then.

The most significant reason that convinced Kaden that he had it bad for Ivy was that, even after a year, it felt right when he wrapped his arm around her, tucking her securely to his side. He believed what he felt for Ivy Linton was the real deal, and it didn't bother him to admit it. The real question was, did she feel the same?

"Kaden, I didn't even bring anything to sleep in. I know it would have been the same at your place because I didn't think about a nightgown, but we would have been alone, and I could get away with sleeping naked."

"I gotcha covered. Just do your thing in the bathroom and come back."

"Kaden..."

"Woman, you have to learn to trust me."

"I used to."

"Tap into that." She nodded unconvincingly. Kaden reached out and brought her close, his lips feeling right on her worried forehead and laying his cheek on her head as they wrapped around each other. "Let me take care of you. Ease into my promise that I will always be here for you."

"I'll try. It's just so much to take in." Ivy lifted her face to his.

"About your mom's friends?"

"More about them coming after me. My mom is self-serving but not hateful. I don't think she would have done this purposely. In her own way, she does love me."

Kaden squeezed her. "I know, but you let me handle the tough stuff. You deal with what you can. Teamwork saves the day."

"Kaden?"

"Hmm?"

"I missed all of this. I missed you. I want more than what we had, but I'm afraid to take that step. I know, I left, it was my fault that we weren't still together, but I'm leery of bringing you all into this mess. Yet, I can't imagine dealing with it alone. It seems like everything I want is still out of reach."

"I know, baby, I missed you too, and I miss the connection we had, but we can build from here. I have to believe we will make it this time."

"I'm not sure I can rely on my instincts after all of this. I mean, I'm trained to see through the subterfuge, but I didn't. What does that say about my skill level?"

"You can't be on high alert all the time. You had to let down your guard at some point. And once you were traumatized, your whole perception changed. You need stability in your life."

"You don't let your guard down. I see you, always watchful, always protective."

"I let my guard down at home and with my friends. Anything could happen once I'm in a relaxed atmosphere. Just like it happened to you." He zeroed in for another kiss, then turned Ivy around and patted her bottom to push her toward the bathroom. "Now, go, get in there."

Watching her as her bottom swayed gently and her curtain of honey gold hair, now longer than a year ago, swung with her movements finishing her sexy picture, he sighed. Kaden's cock was granite hard right now, and he grinned. It had been a long time since his cock got that happy. Half-mast was not unusual but straining to get out, now that had been a memory. Yes, he was glad Ivy came back. He'd worry about her trouble and how to eliminate the problems tomorrow. Tonight, they were in a secure compound, and his arms ached to hold her while they slept.

Kaden turned at the light pat of bare feet as Ivy stood shyly in the bathroom doorway. Their eyes met for a second before she lowered her head, averting her gaze. She appeared vulnerable and uncertain. He got that. Wary he could understand, but his girl was anything but helpless. Kaden hated that she was unsure of herself in any way, but maybe Ivy would share some of the secrets she hadn't shared tonight if she stayed in that emotional state.

Uncertainty with him and about them wasn't good. No, Ivy needed to be confident in who they were as a couple. Time to work on making that a reality. Reminding her who they were before she left was his main goal tonight. Growing stronger to get past that would come. Kaden extended his hand to Ivy, his palm up, inviting her to place her hand into his. And he waited.

Chapter Four

Ivy stared at Kaden's hand, her belly flip-flopping in the memory of what putting her hand in his had previously given her before she ran scared. Warm, sweet love, like heated caramel over ice cream, melted her resolve to keep her secrets. As he wrapped her in all he was, she sensed that he held a corner of himself from her. Could he know that she didn't share all of herself? Probably. Even after this long time apart, Kaden was so in tune with her thinking, how could he miss it?

Not likely that he knew what, exactly, but that she wasn't totally honest, oh, yeah. That explained why he didn't accept her commitment as easily as he had before she'd left him without a word. Before the last year had ripped his heart and then begun to heal the wound she'd left. Ivy felt dirty, like she had sullied what they had by going out with that criminal, JJ. Not dated, she reminded herself, but spent time with someone she knew wasn't a good person. Could feel it.

The realization that she almost destroyed her chance of a normal life with a man so perfect as Kaden brought tears to her eyes. She watched his expression soften further. Ivy took a deep breath. She didn't deserve a man like Kaden, but she would fight to gain his trust and ultimately secure her happiness. His as well, if she believed his words, and she did.

"I know, Ivy. There's more to be said, and it's hard to wrap your mind around everything right now, but all I'm asking for is tonight. Take my hand, let me cradle you and love you with no strings, no thoughts of what we were or what we could be. No worries about yesterday or tomorrow. No thought of right or wrong or the consequences of choices. Just be with me tonight. Can you do that?"

"No expectations? Because earlier, you said if I went home with you, there were."

"No, I meant that, but tonight, we're putting that to the side, no requirements, no commitment past this, here and now. Can you do that? Can you let me love you for just tonight?"

"I can do that."

Ivy walked to Kaden and put her hand in his, her heart swelling with the heat that began to thaw her frozen emotions. Kaden did that to her. The heat in his eyes lit a fire in her, and she felt the icy protective wall surrounding her heart melt. She wouldn't think past now. Tomorrow might hold the end of whatever she and Kaden had, but tonight, she could remember what being with Kaden Trainer was like. What it meant to be content again if she had ever truly been satisfied with anything.

Ivy knew she was thought of as spoiled by most people she dealt with, and she could freely admit she was. Her hair was done weekly, her nails at least twice a month, her makeup was professionally taught and bought. It was easier for her busy parents to buy her things than spend time with her, and soon Ivy became accustomed to the substitution, even convinced herself she preferred it. However, when she met and spent time with Kaden, she realized what she was missing in her life, someone who genuinely cared about her.

Her parents loved her in their own way, sure, but it was a superficial, responsible ownership type of love expressed with trips and trinkets rather than time. Kaden spent time with her. Watched her every move, learned her quirks, and fed her hungry soul with what she didn't even know she longed for, and that was himself.

Kaden didn't lavish her with gifts when they had been together. It was a first for her. Going to private schools, surrounded by wealth, she thought that was typically how one expressed affection. In college, she learned that it was different, in theory, anyway. Soon, she began to practice sending gifts instead of personal attention to her friends and lovers. The gratification was empty. It was too late to be offended by her parents' dysfunctional expression of love, but it wasn't too late to learn how to accept the raw emotion that Kaden offered.

He offered his hand, and she had accepted the offering. A commitment of a kind. Finding that Kaden Trainer was doing very well in his life, job, friendships, and financially was a bonus. It showed her that he was the real deal, unlike the person she had been. If Ivy wanted to gain shelter beneath his umbrella, she would have to change some things. Her level of honesty was the first area to be addressed.

How long she could hide her new information was questionable. Kaden would accept her reticence if she bared her soul now, but later, there was little doubt he'd show her the door. Ivy's eyes met Kaden's, and all thoughts of doing or saying anything profound left her mind. He drew her toward the bed and the tee-shirt laying out on the comforter. The shirt was tossed aside as he drew her to him as he lay down.

Hot, wet lips kissed her neck leaving a path of heat as he scorched his way across her nakedness. Like General Sherman on his march through Georgia, Kaden left no sensitive flesh untouched, no attribute left wanting. She was on fire and desperately needed him to take her to paradise, but after the first rush of passion peaked and subsided, Kaden continued to tease her mercilessly.

Hot hands held her in place as Kaden kissed and suckled her breasts, moving down her midsection to stop only briefly at her navel before progressing to her soft muff. Cognitive thought was leaving her as the next wave of arousal overtook her. That he was magic in and out of bed crossed her mind as she closed her eyes to fall into the pleasure pool.

Kaden watched as Ivy nearly screamed her enjoyment of his methods to relax her. He knew his face carried a teasingly sadistic grin. Until Ivy, he'd never known how sadistic he could be but with a woman who obviously enjoyed her gratification best if either delayed or forced couched in erotic pain, he had grown into the role. Soon, it had become second nature to torment her, gaining more and more information about his girl's limits and secret desires, thereby raising the enjoyment for him and her.

Ivy was hard as nails when it came to her public persona but was soft as silk with him in the bedroom. She was spoiled, and she couldn't hide that even if she had wanted to, which she didn't. Early on, Kaden learned that if he wanted to impress her, he should withhold things she didn't need or genuinely want. He didn't listen to her when she acted in a spoiled whining way. Not that she did it often, and he took her over his knee if she stepped out of bounds.

He might lose her when he implemented the rules and consequences, but when he treated Ivy as a grown woman and not a spoiled, needy brat, things were so much better between them. Discipline, in its many forms, was the key. Kaden had thought they were in a great place relationship-wise, considering it was like a day one do-over, but tonight, she wasn't ready for the intensity life with him entailed.

He wondered if Ivy could deal with her uncertainties and demons enough to let him in completely now. Only time would tell. He knew it wouldn't take much of it to reveal that truth. Tomorrow was early enough to start on the path back to where they were, but tonight he would love her as though nothing had gotten in their way.

As he waited until his girl caught her breath, Kaden made his way back up her lithe body. He appreciated the genetics that created such perfection for him and the athletic life she had led. Horse jumping and Taekwondo did plenty to strengthen her core and give her shapely legs and a butt that had him worshiping at her feet. Maybe she would ride one of Jac's prize-winning beasts while they were here. It would keep her occupied and would burn off some of her nervous energy while he worked on finding and terminating the threat.

Quickly stripping off his jeans and shorts, Kaden bent to lick her ever reddening channel as her arousal increased again. Keeping her sensitive before grabbing her ankles as he rose over her, bringing them to rest on his shoulders, Kaden flicked her clit once and smiled when Ivy twitched.

Wordlessly his eyes drank her perfection briefly, but in those few seconds, he fully appreciated her beauty. She was lightly tanned, glistening with perspiration, and looking at him longingly if not a bit warily. He smiled before plunging into her entrance overflowing with honey and sighed as the first sensations of warmth filled his veins brought on by being sheathed in her heat.

After a few slow cycles of in and out to allow her to orient to him, he hesitated. The thought flashed that he hadn't asked the right questions because he was used to the answers with her, but it had been a year since those answers were relevant.

"Sweetheart, I don't have a condom." He cursed the words even as they left his lips.

"I'm clean, you were my last lover, and I'm still on the pill. Now keep going, for God's sake."

"Yes, ma'am."

He followed that response with a faster-paced attack on her lubricated sex with a steady rhythm, keeping her boobs bouncing and her legs up and parted but not too much. She squeezed her inner muscles, and he nearly blew right then. When she kept up a steady rotation of muscle flexing to compliment his in and out motions, the fire he had only released in the shower for the last year was now building in powerful response.

"Keep it up, woman and I'll have little control. It'll be over fast."

Her little whimper and vaginal grip of his cock told him that was her intention. So be it. Three orgasms were a decent count for a pre-game show, so Kaden concentrated on bringing it all home. Her grunts and whines became heated. Hearing those begging sounds sent his cock into overdrive. The woman was going to kill him.

Bottoming out the second time, his staff bounced off her womb entrance, and he peaked quickly, eyes nearly rolling back into his head. His body took over, and he tried to stretch out the sublime ecstasy by slowing down slightly and rubbing his cock over her sensitive spots. His hand reached down, fingers finding the right placement as he played her one last time. Her muscles rippled again in a lesser climax, alerting Kaden that he had reached the finale.

His strength taxed in a way it hadn't been since he was last with Ivy; he lowered himself in a push-up position over her, kissing her quickly before rolling off and onto the mussed bedding beside her.

"As soon as I've cooled off, I need to take a quick shower. You're welcome to join me." Ivy's satiated giggle brought his smile back. She declined his offer. "Your loss."

"I know," answered Ivy with a yawn. "But I'm tired now."

"Good. My plan worked."

"I'll call on you again when I need to relax."

Kaden chuckled. "At your service, ma'am." His voice became serious. "Always."

IVY AWOKE EARLY AND thought about showering before Kaden got up, but it was so cozy snuggled up to him, his arm thrown over her midsection, that she couldn't make herself move. She could wait to pee a little longer. Last night, he sounded like he was making a vow to always be there for her. If it were only true and if she only deserved his allegiance. She would tackle that later, for now, she inched in just a hair closer and sighed as she closed her eyes to sleep once again.

The sun was in obvious hiding today, the gray skies allowing little light through. There was a storm brewing outside and one brewing inside if the loud voices were any indication. Ivy instinctively knew that one of those voices belonged to Kaden. She wasn't sure about the other, but it might have been Jac's. As though they knew others were listening, the voices became hushed. It brought with it a sense of foreboding.

Nature's demands were too insistent to allow her to lay in bed and figure it out. After she took care of her pressing business, Ivy realized she had never dressed last night. Kaden's tee shirt was lying on the floor beside the bed. Might as well shower and put on her clothes from yesterday. She would have to get her clean things from her car.

A package of undies and socks, four tees, and two pairs of jeans were all she had bought. She didn't want to alert anyone to her flight, so she didn't take any clothes with her, just the essentials. Sharlee had thought on her feet last night when she told Ivy's mom that she was at the competitions. In a more settled world, that is where Ivy would have been, but now she had no idea when her life would be that casual again.

While in the shower, Ivy decided to ask to be taken back to Kaden's. They obviously thought the trouble came from her. She didn't have the heart to put her safety over Kaden's or his friends, even though her mind froze in the terror that she felt when she realized JJ could find her. Would find her. And without Kaden's protection, she would be doomed to a life of servitude if she were lucky.

Remembering the ordeal she had experienced with Ron Cramer-Jones in Montana made her tremble. If it weren't for a group of people, the O'Connors, and Kaden, Jac and Sharlee, she would never have been found, never rescued. And there was no doubt that she would have been sold. Yes, Kaden's group did rescues for a living, but people paid them for those services. Ivy knew how lucky she was to have been brought into their circle.

With this situation, she had possibly, unknowingly tossed Kaden's friends into the fire without agreement. That was unacceptable. A shiver of fear raced along her spine again when Ivy thought of the life she had escaped last night. Horrible. Degrading. Terrifying. How did these things happen to her? Kaden would never make her afraid in the way that JJ's associate Bubba's presence did.

JJ acted as though she should be happy to be in his company, even if Ivy spent it mostly alone. She was something to be owned and admired but not cared for on any intimate level. Kaden made her feel special, like she was worth his time. That was the life she wanted, not one that her mother thought was good. Not like the one with her new husband. Did she dare consider it possible? She was going to do her damnedest.

Charlotte was right when she said these were dangerous people. She would have surely found a connection between the gang and JJ. Ivy had no doubt he was deeply entrenched. Did her mother knowingly set her up with someone in the mob? Ivy knew that her mother never did anything unless she chose to, and going into this marriage was deliberate. More money, position, and power were what she got by marrying Carlton Marciano. Even the name was pretentious. Was he really who Garrett said he was?

Ivy had some decisions to make, and unfortunately, she had a feeling they would need to be made sooner rather than later. Her hunch was right when she stepped out of the shower to Kaden, holding out a towel for her to walk into, his look serious.

"You okay?" she asked.

"Yes, but not so sure about you."

Chapter Five

I vy felt her face draw tight in a frown. Seems like judgment day had arrived sooner than she'd expected. She stepped into the towel and allowed him to wrap her in it. Something was up, and Ivy knew she was soon going to be right behind the eight ball with a cue stick pointed in her direction. Maybe she should cut and run now. They couldn't keep her against her will, right? Make that they wouldn't, would they? Because they very definitely could if they wanted to.

"Ivy baby, what is chasing around in your head?" asked Kaden as he towel-dried her briskly before moving to dry her hair.

"Nothing."

The drying stopped, and he rewrapped her. "Okay, that stops now. Before you get used to lying to me, we need to get a few things straight. The next time I catch you in a lie, you go over my knee. The second time, you go over my knee and take a plug. The third time—"

"I get it, Kaden. Now I remember why I was worried about making this trip. I can't keep anything secret from you. You expect a lot from me. I'm just not sure if it is too much. What if I don't want to bare my soul?"

"We'll negotiate."

"I don't want to put you in the middle of something I can't stop, so before it's too late, I'm leaving. Just take me to my car, and I'll start driving. JJ thinks I'm with you, so until he doesn't think I'm here, I have a chance to get far away. I'll drive north and then south, avoiding Memphis in case he goes there looking for me." As she continued to speak, her anxiety began to grow, and her speech became more pressured and rushed.

Kaden grabbed Ivy and held her tight. "This is just you trying to hide from me that you need to share. This isn't keeping a birthday present secret or some other innocuous thing. It's a worrisome chain of thought that you won't share. I'm not having that between us. I told you I expect better from you. So, what will it be, talk now or I spank your ass until you do? Be assured, this is your one and only get out of jail free opportunity, Ivy. Make it count. To be honest, I hope you don't use it."

"No, I'm trying to steer trouble away from you, all of you."

"Really? Martyrdom doesn't suit you. It's the wrong way to do it. I told you if you leave, it will be after we have an honest conversation. Unless you are ready to be totally honest, you're going nowhere."

Kaden knew that would drive Ivy mad. When she got into one of her defiant moods, she did the exact opposite of what was expected, and he was sure disclosing that ignoring him was exactly what he wanted would either push her to do the right thing or give him a chance to smack that luscious, rebellious bottom. Something he had wanted to do since she left him last year. Something he had promised her last night before all hell broke loose.

Kaden knew he was pushing hard, but a lot was riding on this, and the more that Charlotte dug, the deeper the shit went.

Jac had just handed him his ass for allowing Ivy to withhold information. He was right. Complete honesty was the minimum Kaden would ever require, and it was time to remind his girl. He'd allowed Ivy to withhold things in the hope that she would tell him on her own. She hadn't. Now it was his turn.

Besides, it was a lesson she needed to learn now because he had no intention of letting Ivy out of his life again. They might as well start things off the way they intended to live, with no secrets. Her playing the martyr was not going to work.

Still wrapped in the towel, he held her close and enjoyed her sweet scent. It wasn't the herbal bath gel that excited him, although that had a nice aroma; it was the citrus and hay that he always detected as her own personal scent that made him smile. He never noticed any other woman had an essence about her, but it was immediately recognizable with Ivy. Sharlee called it pheromones, and Kaden was glad he could detect Ivy's.

He pushed her damp hair away from her face. "Sweetheart, it will be okay, but right now, I need to remind you there are ground rules to being with me. Especially when you're in hot water."

"Am I?"

He almost believed she wasn't sure. "Oh yes, my naughty one, you certainly are. Now time's up. Talk."

He wanted nothing more than to take her under him again and tease her, then possess her, but they had work to do to get to the bottom of this mess. Charlotte had mentioned that it might be tied to the office building explosion and subsequent collapse. No one thought that Ivy had anything to do with the bombing, but she might have been the reason. He might have been the reason. Everyone had a signature, and they might have found Marciano's.

The mob might have tried to cut her off from her last support. Kaden himself. It was becoming clear they had decided they wanted her, likely that JJ character. It was normal business to get rid of any potential barriers to their success. Because Ivy's mother was so accommodating, and Ivy had years of getting her own way, the modern-day gang likely thought they would get what they wanted from both women simply by pandering to their whims.

Maybe they hadn't decided exactly what that would be, or maybe JJ wanted a trophy wife who said nothing and looked good on his arm. There could be many reasons they had chosen Ivy, but they wanted her... of that, he was sure. They wouldn't get her. Of that, he was equally sure.

No answer from his girl. So be it. Kaden began to walk to the bed with Ivy in tow.

"No, Kaden. Please don't get mad. I don't know what you want me to say. My mom set me up with JJ. She encouraged the rides with him. The couple of dinners he provided on those rides were not dates. I didn't agree to be with him as together, just as grabbing a bite to eat. Why he wanted to be with me was a mystery. He never tried anything, really."

"So why does he have you tracked?"

"I don't know that he did, really."

"Oh, he did. I can guess why, but how is the real question."

Either they had figured out her value to them or were sore losers and wanted her back. While Ivy had showered, Kaden had taken her purse to Carter, but there wasn't a bug in there. She could have changed purses, so not a reliable place to plant it. Not in her pack either, Levi checked. That left her car or her person. Since he had her naked and there were no tattoos or implants that he had seen, he couldn't figure it out.

He fingered her necklace. "Do you ever take this pendant off?"

Her hand came up in a protective move, covering his fingers and the necklace. "No. My dad gave this to me."

"I remember. Just wondering if JJ could have gotten to it."

"No. I took it off once to have a mole removed from my shoulder, but my mom held it for me, and I got it back the next day."

"I wondered what that was on your shoulder. I assumed it was a cut. Pretty new scar."

"A few months back."

Kaden kissed the spot and held back his smile of satisfaction when she shivered. "So, she was already married."

"Yes, but why does that matter?"

He lifted the pendant off her neck and turned it around. "It's a cameo."

"Yes, hey, if you wanted to know what was inside, you just had to ask me," complained Ivy as he popped it open.

Inside was a picture of her and her dad but over her father's picture was a little chip. "Found it." Kaden slipped it out of position and let it land in his palm. "This little chip is your homing device of sorts. They can track you practically anywhere." Ivy stared at the little bit of plastic and metal in Kaden's big hand and then looked into his eyes. "Still think there isn't anything going on?"

Ivy seemed to deflate. "I don't think my mom did that."

"No, probably not, but did she know? Maybe. The thing is, baby, you are in danger, and we have to get you out of it."

"But I don't know what I did."

"You didn't have to do anything. Gangs are opportunistic. They see you; they are given access to you, then they use you. The thing is, you can't do something for them and get out easily. You're trapped."

"Kaden, stop scaring me. Look, if that is the case, if what you are telling me is true and they have picked me, I need to get away from you, from everyone."

Kaden drew Ivy into his arms, holding tightly as he spoke into her hair. "You're mine, remember? Unless you don't want me, then that issue is settled. I protect what is mine and don't think that there aren't plenty of things we can do to break their very tenuous hold on you. But I can't do anything if you don't stay and talk to me."

"Kaden..."

"Ivy, please stay."

Ivy turned into his flannel shirt and inhaled his clean, masculine scent. "Are you sure?"

"As sure as I can be, more than I have ever been sure about anything else. It won't always be easy with me, but you will always be loved."

"You love me?"

"You didn't know that?" Ivy shook her head. "You left thinking I didn't love you?"

"I didn't think it was soon enough for you to love me. I'm not even sure what being in love feels like."

"You will. Or maybe you do but are expecting something else. You'll know when the time is right. I promise you."

"Isn't that a problem?"

"What? You not being sure about your feelings? Nope, because I'm sure."

The couple stood a few more moments, enjoying each other's presence. Warm, firm lips began to travel down her cheek, leaving a trail of heat. Ivy lifted her head to meet his descent to her lips. She fell into the sensation of tenderness he began with, then her libido met his insistent kisses. She opened her mouth slightly in an attempt to drag in some much-needed air. Breathing through her nose was not enough.

Kaden took that opportunity to plunder her inner sanctum, his tongue twirling with hers in a mimic of the mating dance. Heavy, frantic kisses and taking hard breaths between his pillaging drove Ivy to raise one leg to his waist. Kaden, not to miss a cue, grabbed both of her thighs and held them around his hips as she climbed him like a tree. His hands moved to support her ass as his kissing and loving consumed every thought.

Ivy could feel her body move of its own accord, and if she were less aroused, she might have become embarrassed at her dry humping him, but she wasn't. She vaguely acknowledged he was moving when her back met the mussed bedding. Kaden reached down to unzip and quickly divested himself of his pants and underwear together.

He palmed his manhood a few times and then zeroed in on her dripping entrance. Without a word of preparation, Kaden plunged deeply, forcing a grunt from his lips and an answering one from hers. Sounds of wet flesh slapping wet flesh combined with little noises of need sounded throughout the bedroom.

"Touch yourself."

Ivy wasted no time following his direction as he continued to slide along her sensitive vaginal walls, now trembling with little ripples of response. "I'm nearly there, honey."

"I'm right with you. More, I need more, Kaden." He obliged.

Sweat rolled down his face as Ivy could hear herself get louder. "Come for me, baby, but no sound. Hear me? Quiet." That did it. Ivy's muscled vagina clamped on Kaden's staff and practically drew his orgasm from him. She let out a low whine but nothing else as she peaked hard.

Kaden watched as she slowly floated to earth. He felt as she looked, ethereal. Satisfied. Sated. He wanted nothing more than to keep her in bed with him all day, but duty called. He had to spank her ass to keep his word to her and encourage her disclosures to come more freely. Then shower, show Carter the tracker and get Ivy to breakfast. He dropped a kiss on her cheek coated lightly with perspiration.

Reluctant because of the timing but anticipating the act, he repositioned and drew Ivy over his naked thighs. At least this time, his staff wouldn't be pushing up against her from the arousal that spanking her always brought him.

"Kaden, what are you doing?"

He laughed. "Is that the real question?"

"No, why are you doing this?"

"Promised you last night, but I put it off. I had intended to come in this morning and heat your ass first and then go forward, but you were in the shower, and then you turned me around like you always do. Now, however, I am keeping my word, even if it's out of order. I owe you a hot bottom for taking off and leaving me for a year with no contact. And now you have earned more because you are still keeping secrets."

The first round of smacks to her bottom raised a squeal, and her legs went flying in the air. "I told you to be quiet. People will hear you."

"Don't you think they will hear you slapping my ass?"

"Good point."

"Then stop."

"Nope." Kaden rained down a flurry of swats on Ivy's bottom, searing her rear to a perfect rare color. "You lied to me, Ivy and that will never do." The smacks came fast, hard, and were relentless. Nothing sexy about the heat he was laying on her bottom. "Do you have some truths you need to share with me?"

"No. I swear."

"If that's what you want to stand by."

Crying out and more pleading continued as he shifted Ivy to put her lower cheeks on display. "You left me without talking first, and you tried to leave me again without our agreement. I don't care what your reasoning is; we are discussing all major decisions."

The cries became more intense, and then it happened, what always happened if he spanked hard enough and long enough, Ivy became aroused again. She still whimpered, but it was mixed with moans and then she arched her back and presented her ass herself. Like a cat in heat, his girl was asking for the spanking.

"Spread your legs, Ivy."

She complied instantly, her core slippery from intercourse and from new arousal. Her honey was sliding down her legs and onto him. He scooped his two fingers in her wetness and positioned her on the edge of the bed, knowing she expected something different than what she was about to get.

"Get in position, naughty girl." She hadn't forgotten. She quickly got on her knees, arched her back and spread her legs. "Show me."

Ivy hesitated just a moment before reaching back and spreading her back cheeks, exposing her anus. Such a pretty starburst. He lubed her back entrance with her arousal and then re-lubed his fingers before, slowly and gently but with steady force, pushed past her sentry muscle guarding the entrance and, once breached, continued inserting to his fingers' hilt. Two was all he would do today. Gently scissoring his digits as his girl began pumping back and forth against them. He simply held his fingers firm as she did the fucking.

He slapped her butt every few rotations to heighten her frenzy. Then he did what he wasn't going to do, he introduced three. She stopped, and he slapped her butt.

"Keep going, or I will do it."

When she still hesitated, he pushed in the three fingers and flicked her clit. She began to take up the rhythm again, slower this time, but she didn't stop again.

"I have to come, Kaden. Please let me come." She remembered.

"Should naughty girls get to come?"

Ivy panted, "No, sir. But please. I ache so much."

"Are you going to tell us everything you know about these people?"

"Yes, I'll tell you, but I don't know much."

"I'm spanking your pussy, then you can come."

"Oh, but it will hurt."

"Yep, and put you over. Either I do it, or we stop now, and I finish your spanking the old- fashioned way. No coming. Now ask me, and don't slow down." His alpha voice was her undoing. It always was the last straw.

Her raspy voice pleaded. "Please spank my pussy, sir."

"Hard," he prompted.

"Hard."

"Good girl. Now start pumping faster."

Kaden knew she'd be sore, but he didn't have a plug right now. This would have to do. He reached down with his other hand, and just as she reseated her ass on his fingers, he slapped her sopping wet pussy. The sensitivity of his girl made her cry out, but she didn't stop moving.

"Now again." And as he finished his last word, he slapped.

"Sir, sir. I can't..."

"One more."

The wet splat was heard, and she climaxed in the same few seconds, pounding her ass against his fingers. His other hand moved quickly up to her clit and pinched then twiddled her. As she began to slow to a near stop, Kaden removed his fingers from her ass and kissed her upturned, sweaty bottom. Placing a hickey on her butt, he well and truly marked his girl. She was his, and there would be no more discussion.

As she settled down from her last burst of fireworks, he kissed up her back.

"I'm showering quickly, baby. You can jump in, but it's five minutes only. We have things to do." Five minutes should be enough to rinse off and jack off, he thought.

As they dressed, Kaden admired how Ivy had her dressing routine down so well, she had cleaned up, fixed her hair, put on make-up, and dressed in fifteen minutes. She looked like it had taken much longer than that.

As he pulled on his trusty cowboy boots, he said nonchalantly, "I forgot you were noisy when you get excited."

"Kaden Trainer, I was quiet."

"Today but last night..." he shook his head and laughed at the horrified expression on her face.

"Are you kidding me? Everyone heard us?"

"Not everyone, just the people who slept here last night."

"Which was Jac and Sharlee."

"And the security people."

She grinned. "It gave them something to talk about today."

Kaden laughed. "I'm sure it did."

Downstairs, Kaden handed the tracking device to Carter, who was polishing off what was likely his second breakfast. "In her necklace. My money is on Carlton Marciano, about two months ago. Even before that Jester character made himself available to her."

Sharlee spoke. "That makes sense. They were grooming her, except she wasn't taking the training well, I would guess."

"Nope. Never does." He grinned at Ivy's huff of protest. "But for some reason, they don't want to let go. We need to find out why."

"I'm on it after I check with Finley about the schedule today. Who would have figured a former marine drill sergeant would make a good nanny?"

When Sharlee left the room, Jac said nonchalantly, "Security reports two SUV's doing a slow drive-by at sporadic intervals making themselves known but not advancing. They have raised the security level and have taken preventative measures. We will be kept updated."

Kaden grunted and shook his head. No response from the others. Jac was quiet until Ivy served herself some breakfast and sat next to Carter. Kaden sat on the other side. "So, Ivy, any thoughts on why they want you?"

"No. I don't know what business Carlton has. He told me he's in investment banking. I certainly don't have any idea about that."

Mark laughed. "Is that what they're calling it now? Jessie will love hearing about that."

"Seems to me there's something. Maybe you saw something." Ivy looked up to see if he had information he wasn't sharing, but Jac just took the last bite of his eggs. "You eat, and then we will get to work trying to figure things out." Jac stood without waiting for an affirmative from Ivy.

"Is he always that bossy?" Ivy whispered.

Kaden smiled. "No, he's worse when things don't go his way, or life throws a curveball."

Ivy answered his smile with one of her own, but she didn't feel it. She was never sure about Jac. He gave the impression of being simple and straightforward, but anyone who had spent half an hour with the man knew he was anything but simple. She sensed he went deep, incredibly deep.

Ivy didn't feel like smiling after they started to go through what Charlotte had found, either. By the end of the morning, Ivy's brain was spinning. Her mother married the head of a branch of the Indianapolis Mafia family, therefore, totally immersed in La Cosa Nostra. They were now in Lexington. What that meant exactly, Ivy didn't know, but it wasn't good.

In court, it had come out that Ron Cramer-Jones, convicted murderer and Ivy's kidnapper, had done jobs for that family. Probably how they knew about her. He wasn't a member of the Marciano family, but it had been obvious when he held her captive that he had no trouble with kidnapping, killing, theft, and whatever else he had done.

Ivy wondered why her mother never changed her last name, now she had a good idea. She stayed in Lexington while her new husband traveled for business, but sometimes he stayed at the house for several weeks. Ivy figured that he was hiding out at those times. Her imagination was running wild, and even though Charlotte had more to research, it was enough for Ivy.

Before she acknowledged what her brain had told her body, Ivy was leaving the room where everyone was gathered, and if it weren't for Kaden pulling her into his arms and continuing away from the group, Ivy might never have noticed she'd left.

Kaden hugged her. "I'm sorry about that. It's a lot to take in, honey. Do you need a break?"

"Can I go for a ride?"

"What? Don't you want to talk about it?"

"No. I absolutely do not want to talk about it right now. I want to forget I'm tangled in this monstrosity of a mess. I want to feel free. I can do that if I ride."

"Do you want me to go with you?"

"Not really. I want to ride hard and fast. You don't like riding."

"Let me get Jac. He can tell you which one you can ride."

A few moments later, Kaden returned with Jac, both carrying on a subdued but serious conversation. "I hear you want to ride. I know you grew up around horses but remind me how well you ride."

"I trained them, did barrel racing and jumped for a few years. I even rode dressage for a year. I know my horses and my limits."

"Yes, but you don't know mine. Tell you what. I'll ride with you for a short bit, see how you do, and then, if I'm comfortable, I'll leave you to it."

"Honestly, Jac, I'm fine alone."

"Probably, but it's my only offer."

"Whatever."

"You need a spanking."

"Thanks, but I'm sure you know it's already been an event today."

"Good to hear, but I'd remember there are no limits to how many times a man can take care of business. Your things are upstairs in the bedroom, so you can change, and I'll change. We'll meet back here in, say, ten minutes?"

"Yes. That works."

Kaden returned to the strategy session while his girl got rid of the cobwebs. It was going to be a long week.

Chapter Six

After several minutes of riding and talking, Jac asked, "When did you first meet Marciano?"

"Maybe six months ago? I'm not sure. I don't see my mother often. I live in one of the manager houses, and she lives in our family home."

"Is that because of the kidnapping?"

"Partly. Partly because once my father died, she began dating a lot. I thought she got over his death too quickly. I still do. She married less than two years after the death of a man she said she loved deeply. If I lost Kaden... anyway. I just gave her a wide berth."

"After you met, how long before they were engaged."

"Oh, I didn't meet Carlton until they were engaged."

"Ah."

"Yes, and before you ask, I did say something about it, but since she was determined it was who she was going to marry, I stepped back and stayed away until the wedding. That's where I met JJ. He took me home after the wedding. He was a gentleman but cool, entitled. I know I must seem that way to other people, and I'm sure I felt that way for much of my growing up, but now, after my recent experiences, I don't. I'm thankful for the good things in my life."

"And Kaden?"

"What about Kaden?"

"Charlotte tells me her best friend is into you on a visceral level."

"Is he? So he tells me, but I'm not easy to be with on some days."

Jac chuckled. "How about you?"

"I'm fairly sure I've fallen head over heels, but I need to keep my wits about me right now, so I'm going cautiously. I don't want to make another mistake, and I think if I rush this, it could be just that."

"I thought that about Charlotte. She changed my mind."

"Kaden has told me a little. But you two worked together, got to know each other in all areas. Sharlee was an integral part of your team. I'm just an appendage that is not usually helpful and often annoying."

"Is that how you see yourself? Unnecessary?"

"In this scenario, and to Kaden's life, yes. I mean, he does care about me, I know that, but I cause more trouble than I'm worth. I haven't been very productive in my life. I intended to change that, but I just never seem to get there."

"Then change that. I can guarantee Kaden would not agree."

"I'm trying, but just when it seems like I might be on a good path, something happens, like that kidnapping. I had started work on my dance and martial arts studio. I was already helping a few clients per week learn different aspects of horse riding and expedition. Now I was about to start up again when this happened. Maybe I'm not meant to be completely fulfilled as a person. It's a profession or a love life."

"Sounds like a bunch of excuses for not putting your nose to the grindstone and get things done. If you want it bad enough, you can do all you need to be fulfilled and have a happy home life. You could even get that Ph.D. and come to work for me."

"Doing what, exactly? I don't think you would want me to psycho-analyze your people."

"Why not? It's a tough job. When something happens on the job that might shake a team member up, I need to make sure that there is someone I can use that will be invested in their dealing with the shit and be discreet. I do have more than one team, you know. And I hire new people as I need them, or they present themselves to me. It's a damn good idea. Consider it."

When Jac says to consider something, he isn't giving you a choice; it's a command. She imagined his troops didn't question him often when commanding soldiers or in the civilian world.

"I'm not sure I want it all bad enough. I don't follow through easily."

"I know Kaden pretty well, and he will help you with that."

"See, more trouble."

Again, Jac went silent. This time, Ivy didn't try to fill the empty space with explanations. She knew the drill. She waited him out like the psychologist she was trained to be. Jac led Ivy to a racetrack on his land. Once inside the gate, he began to put the standardbred through his paces. Ivy followed suit on her quarter horse.

The wind pulled at her hair and whipped across her face, taking her breath away. The exhilaration was amazing and familiar. She lowered her body to streamline the airflow and reveled in the freedom. Slowing to a more sustainable pace and then ultimately meeting up with a now walking duo, Ivy settled beside the man and his mount.

"You're good," admired Ivy.

"You're a skilled rider as well. I expected you to be this good. It isn't why I insinuated myself on this ride."

"I figured."

Jac grinned. "I wanted to see how deep you were in with the Marcianos. I'm a military man. We are all military men, but since leaving the service, we want to believe in what we do. We have to start work in earnest again next week. We have new jobs, so I have to make sure my people are safe when we do them. Ideally, I'd like to wrap up the information gathering and the strategic part of this gig before we move on.

"It is most important that I know what I need to do to keep my family and my people from being overrun by Marciano. We have connections and can use them if needed. I'll be honest, if I had even an inkling that you were here under false pretenses, because let's face it, your timing was a little too perfect, I would have had you dumped in the Kentucky River."

Ivy had to process what he was really saying. He would have disposed of her and the threat she carried. She'd known Jac and his own band of merry men were often hired on high profile contracts, but mercenary work? She'd been clueless.

"So, you're mercenaries."

"Nope, a security company. But we are used to special detachment duty."

"Meaning black ops?"

"Meaning we know how to neutralize the enemy, of which you are not."

"Maybe I am. JJ or someone tracked me to Kaden's condo and got inside the building somehow, putting him in danger."

"And you."

"Yes, and me, but I don't matter the same. I brought it with me. Now they've followed me here if your gate security is right."

"They're right. I'm still not sure how much you can deal with right now. You're the only one, besides my son, who isn't paid to do a job that is also in my inner circle. It's a new experience for me, and we'll have to take it slow. So, you let us worry about Marciano and Company for now. You worry about following Kaden's lead. In my world, the non-operative relies on the operative.

"And don't ever think this is anything else but our own version of a family. Our women do their jobs, have their lives, but the minute they are told to do something to save themselves, they do it. Don't force Kaden to take whatever action is necessary to keep you safe because you chose to refuse his direction. It puts everyone at risk. We have methods of correction when that happens. I believe you are quite familiar with several of those methods."

Ivy didn't respond, and Jac didn't elaborate on what those methods were. They both knew. Monroe even bragged he carried a rubber paddle as one method. She suspected it was talk for keeping mouthy women in line, but she had no real proof either way. Ivy suspected Monroe was a deeper man than she realized, and his rubber paddle and talk of spanking was a cover, but just in case, she was keeping a little bit of cautious distance between him and her.

Later, she and Kaden had eaten dinner with the others, and not a person mentioned the ride she and Jac had taken, including Kaden. She imagined they all knew what they covered on that ride but not her answers to those things. It wasn't their business. Jac was a hard man with many responsibilities that he obviously took seriously, but he was as pliable as pulled taffy around his wife and son. She wanted that with Kaden. She knew she was the roadblock to having it.

There were many things that Ivy could have done instead of deciding to stay at Jacquard and Charlotte Reynaud's home, but two days later, she didn't regret the choice. Several turning points brought her to the decision to remain with Kaden, surrounded by these people in this situation. Kaden never doubted it because he said "good" like it was only her that had debated it.

The first deciding point, obviously, was her desire to rekindle her relationship with Kaden Trainer. Kaden was the one she couldn't get out of her mind or heart and the one who made her stand on her own. He encouraged her to be independent and yet yield to his dominance. He wanted her to tell her truth and then be silent for his. It had been difficult, but she could and would do it to keep Kaden.

That protection felt good, actually. Kaden was secure and bossy, but he was predictable in how he dealt with life and her. If Ivy held herself back from him because she was in a mood, which she had often been during the time she'd been back with Kaden, he enacted his brand of punishment. If she did as he asked, or was asked, he rewarded her. It sounded like Kaden Trainer was a man who fit his name, but Ivy didn't feel like one of Pavlov's dogs. She was actually content. Her one worry was being found by Marciano's people. They hadn't laid eyes on her, and now that the tracker was destroyed, they couldn't be sure where she was, but the fear she had was real.

It had been a testy few days, but Ivy was at the place where she could comfortably say Kaden was probably her one and only. The man she would always regret not staying with if she ever left. The one she would look for if he ever left her. The man she would never get over nor understand completely. Kaden, unlike any other significant person in her life, had rules and expectations. That adventure excited her.

The second moment of truth in her decision to hang tough and let this group take care of the mess she had been forced to land was Jac Reynaud himself. Jac had ridden out with her that first day to see how well she could ride. That was his excuse. His true reason was to feel her out on where she actually stood in the whole mafia, crime family realm. He'd asked some straightforward questions that afternoon and was obviously satisfied with the answers because she was suddenly treated as more of an insider than an outsider. He'd made her examine her own motives and expectations of herself. Hard truths were always difficult to acknowledge, but she had and even mulled over his offer to work for him if she got off her butt and went that last step.

The third reason was she was scared. She'd met Bubba, seen his associates, and had felt dirty afterward. The same kind of dirty she'd felt from Carlton but for a different reason. Bubba was open about his sleaziness. Carlton tried to hide it beneath his overly friendly smiles, sleek manners, and indulgences that he obviously thought hid the true man inside. It hadn't.

What the Marciano family might have done was destroy the office building that held Kaden and his group, the only ones who could put an end to them getting Ivy in their clutches. It seemed as though it was Jac's family protecting their own against the Marciano family. And didn't that just give her a sick feeling? But they were confident, so she was learning to be confident.

"What's that overactive brain thinking now?" asked Kaden as he crawled into bed next to her.

"That I don't want to get anyone killed."

"I know. Honestly, I think we have decided that Marciano had something to do with the building destruction. The bomb used was the exact type of bomb used in two other similar but lesser attacks that the feds had previously assigned to his group. I don't think they did it because of you or me specifically. It was just a nice bonus for them. Jac has had some dealings with enough people to have stepped on their toes. We have a good idea of what the true target was and are working on that. Right now, we're still planning while we watch and wait."

Kaden reached for Ivy like he did every night. He cuddled her as they worked through the business of strategy. If Kaden was on the computer, he placed a chair next to his so their legs would touch as he worked, and she watched or played on her phone. He was so demonstrative that it embarrassed her a little, but Kaden was no more or less than Carter, Mark or Jac. She didn't know about the other women, but she stayed aroused nearly all day. By the time they went to bed, she was nearly incinerated with the fire inside.

"Charlotte has gotten so much information we're nearly drowning in it. We should have a plan completed tomorrow.

I thought they would cover their tracks better than they did. And I thought they'd make their move to recover you. Something is up, but I don't know what it is, exactly."

"Or maybe Sharlee is better than most."

"She is that. Now no more talking about how good others are when you're in bed with me," Kaden chided in mock offense.

"Hmm, maybe you should show me how good you are, you know, refresh my memory."

"Sounds like an excellent plan," agreed Kaden as he rolled Ivy on top of him.

Leaning down to kiss Kaden deeply, her hands roaming his nakedness, while he did the same. Ivy squealed at the pounding on the door. Kaden, who was enjoying the foreplay as much as she was, immediately rolled her to the space between the bed and the wall and had the bedside drawer open and was holding his gun before Ivy even realized what the pounding was.

"Trainer, get dressed. Code black."

"Kaden?"

"Listen, baby, do as I say. Get dressed, put on your shoes, grab your coat, cell, charger, and bag, then sit in here until I come back for you. If you need to, hide here, beside the bed."

As he spoke, he had already pulled out more weapons and was strapping up his body armor and gear before covering the whole in completely black clothing. He smudged his face with black grease. It all took less than a few minutes.

"I'm going with you."

"No, you aren't. This isn't a game, Ivy. You stay here until one of us comes for you. I don't expect to be gone long, but you bundle up and sleep in that corner if I am. Understand me? Do not leave this room alone." Kaden's eyes showed darker with face paint on. His dom voice was heavy with warning.

"I'm scared."

"I know, but this place is a fortress. The grounds just need flushing of the vermin. I'll be back soon. Promise you will do as I said."

"I promise."

Kaden was gone. Ivy wasn't sure what was going on, but she had a good idea. Sharlee would be in on the computers and doing surveillance. Her baby was likely in a lockdown with Finley somewhere. When she had first heard that little Storm Reynaud had a former marine nanny, she'd laughed. Finley could take care of any threat. Kaden had said he would keep that in mind if and when they ever had kids.

A kick-ass nanny could take care of the home front just fine if Kaden were away. Now, she wondered if they could get one for her. She'd share when she and Kaden had children. And that little fantasy made her feel better.

Don't get ahead of yourself. Ivy thought about the danger and knew that this group was well prepared to protect them all and take out the threats. Somehow, even with the violence that might be going on outside, she felt much safer here than in the rest of the world.

Ivy checked the clock and saw it had only been half an hour since Kaden left. It felt like hours. Just as she sat back on the side of the bed, preparing to settle in to wait for however long it was going to take, the floor vibrated like a small earthquake had just happened. The sound that accompanied it was not at all from a natural disruption. It was from a manmade explosive. A voice came over a hidden intercom of some sort.

"Ivy, this is Sharlee. The guys are fine. I'm monitoring them. Some idiot tried to blow up the gate. It missed. The guys have all the trespassers but one captured. Looks like it won't be long before they run the last one down. As soon as they have cleared the mess, the cops will come and take away the uninvited guests and then the guys will be back. I'll tell you when it's clear to come down to the den."

"A-all right. Thank you."

It didn't sound fine, but what could Ivy do but believe Sharlee. It took a while, but when Sharlee gave the all-clear, Ivy didn't hesitate. She quickly went downstairs, and after taking the offered glass of wine, she sat in the corner of one sofa and anxiously awaited Kaden's return. It was just Sharlee and Ivy because Jessie and Becky and their men went home after dinner. The others, Levy, Garrett, and Monroe, stayed, likely expecting a scenario like this.

The guys finally came back in, dirty, tired, and somber. It all seemed a little scary, so Ivy stayed still and didn't say a word. Jac must have not seen her at first because he started talking to Sharlee.

"I took snaps of the guys here tonight. I think I recognized a few, so can you pull up our hall of famers and let's see what we have?"

"I'll pull up the list, but I'm not working on it tonight. It's two a.m."

The two continued to talk and banter between themselves as the others drifted off to bed. Ivy honed her attentions on the couple, hoping to get a look at the faces of the men Jac's team had found on the grounds.

"It's time you go to bed too."

"Ahh!" Ivy's hand shot to her chest, and she sucked in the air dramatically. "You startled me."

"Sorry. Thought you knew I was here. I have a job to do tomorrow and need to get some sleep. You can hear all about things in the morning."

Ivy looked into the blackened face. "After you take a shower."

Kaden grinned. "Not into my new look?"

"To be honest," she grinned back, "I like a more clean and neat appearance."

"Let's go. This isn't my favorite look either." When she hesitated, Kaden leaned down to give Ivy a grease kiss, and with a subdued squeal, she raced from the room. Kaden followed, calling good night to their hosts as he left the room with a chuckle.

Chapter Seven

The next morning Kaden was gone when Ivy got up, but he had said he on a job today. It was a little awkward without her defender, and she missed the little touches, but this was how it would often be once life got back to normal. Ivy hoped it wasn't anything that would put him in danger, but of course, she knew that was his line of work. She still wasn't sure what his line was exactly, but so long as he came home to her whole and unharmed, she guessed it didn't matter. Much.

As she walked downstairs to find out what the whole story about last night was, her surprise at seeing Kaden was obvious. "Hey, I thought you were working today."

"I'm working every day, but Levi took my place so I could be here for this morning. I'll get you some coffee and an omelet. We just finished eating, and there's plenty left."

"I don't usually eat so much."

"I'd say you don't usually eat enough, but that's for another day. I'll give you just the omelet and no toast or potatoes, deal?"

"Yes." She lifted her face to Kaden's kiss and sat at the table.

Monroe sat next to her. "Ready for the real fun to begin?"

"Pardon?"

"We've identified each person caught last night when we were playing war games. I think you might know a few of them."

"Me? How would I know them?"

Kaden put her plate in front of her with a small glass of orange juice. "Oh, I don't drink juices."

"You will today."

Kaden was in a dominant mood this morning, and Ivy had spent enough time with him to know when compliance was mandatory and advisable. Today was one of those days. She said nothing.

Garrett walked over to grab more coffee. "She's learning. I'll go set things up. Sharlee should be ready soon."

"We'll be there in a few," said Kaden as Monroe stood to follow Garrett.

"Mark and Carter are bringing the women. It's time to move into our new digs, but we need to get the debriefing done before then. When we move, and if we think you're safe enough, we will go back to the condo. How does that sound?"

"Heavenly."

"Good. We will have extra security now, so it should be fine."

"Kaden, I can't be surrounded all the time or live in the middle of bells and whistles and cameras."

"Ivy, I know it's hard, but whatever it takes to keep you safe is what I'll do. Now finish eating."

"I'm not through talking about this."

"I know, but we have more important things to get through first."

As they walked into the room, filled with most of Kaden's team, along with Becky and Jessie, Ivy was immediately on alert. Everyone was looking at the pictures projected on the wall. Ivy stilled at Bubba's big, angry face and a handful of the guys at his Kingdom Games.

"That's Bubba's crew. Not all of them but the meaner ones."

"But no JJ?" prompted Sharlee.

She looked at all the faces again. "No."

"Ivy, are you sure Bubba was the leader?"

"Yeah, I mean, no one said it, but everyone did what he said."

"Even JJ?"

"Well, I assumed it was Bubba who called him all the time but, actually, I never heard them talk together except when I met him and one other time."

"When was that second time?" asked Jac.

Ivy hesitated, but Kaden urged, "Baby?"

She turned her repentant face to Kaden. "When I left in the Uber to get my car, just before coming here. I passed his open door when I was leaving the building."

Ivy sat down, and Kaden stood next to her. "It's why you came, isn't it?"

"No, I was going to come after telling JJ not to call me again, then call you. I know I can't prove I called now that your office is gone, but it's the truth."

Becky spoke up. "Actually, I accessed our phones and messages. I can verify that Ivy called looking for you, Kaden, four times in one hour the day before and three times the day she got here."

"Okay. But why then, why now?"

"Besides the fact that I missed you and my conversation with Molly."

"Yes."

"There is something you don't know. I'm afraid to tell you."

"I don't understand why. I can't believe you withheld information after we have asked you, *I* have asked you," said Kaden, his voice gruff with his irritation.

"Kaden, if you don't believe me, then why am I going to tell the only thing I have as a bargaining chip to staying alive?"

"Dammit. Go ahead, tell us what you have hidden this whole week." Kaden still wasn't appeased by her words, and Ivy could feel him slip through her fingers even before she told what she knew.

"For survival, Kaden. You saw what these people can do. Now I know why they can do it. I don't have the heavy artillery you do or the skills to kill someone with my bare hands or sneak up on them before they know you're there. I have some martial arts training. That's it."

Kaden shook his head and sat down next to her, grabbing her hands firmly. "I'm not sure how to deal with us, but right now, we need to know the rest, Ivy."

She nodded, speaking only to Kaden. "Everything I said up to the day JJ offered to take me to my car was as I told you. I didn't know anything about any of them or their connection to organized crime until you all told me. I didn't like JJ or his group and tried to distance myself from them, but it didn't work. My mom kept bringing him in when I would be around, and in a crowd, I couldn't be rude. I think she was also trying to keep me safe in her own way, but who knows." Ivy finished her statement with a shrug.

Garrett drew her attention from Kaden. "What happened the day he took you to get the car, honey."

Ivy turned in Garrett's direction, his kindness settling her more than Kaden at that moment. The words began to flow of their own volition, her mind drawing her back to that fateful day.

"My mom set it up for JJ to take me to get my car from the shop. I didn't know about it, or I would have already left, but he was there and offering, so I had little choice but to accept. He has a way of making you do things his way. It's as though you have no option but to comply. Anyway, he got a call when we were on our way. He told me he had to make a stop but would be out quickly."

"That's when you waited for him," supplied Monroe.

"Yes, but the problem was he wasn't ready to go after half an hour, so I got up to look for him. This is where the story is different. I tried to find him and couldn't, at first. I rounded a corner and headed down a hallway because I thought I could hear him talking to someone. When I called out as I came to the doorway, I must have surprised him. He was with a man you haven't shown me a picture of yet. They were arguing, and when JJ heard me, he looked up. The fury in his eyes was deadly."

Ivy took a breath and tried to push away the memory of that face, those eyes, and the terror they evoked in her. A warm arm came around her upper body, and Kaden's scent surrounded her. He kissed her temple.

"It's okay, baby. No one can get to you. JJ is never going to touch you."

"You mean again?"

The arms tightened for a few seconds before releasing their intensity. Kaden answered through clenched teeth. "Yes. Tell me what you mean."

"I had only heard a smattering of what was said, and I don't know if JJ was angry that I went looking for him or that I found him, but he grabbed my arm and yanked me out of the room, tossing me against the hallway wall. Not really hard, but it scared me when it looked like he wanted to hit me. He refrained."

Kaden stood abruptly and paced the space in front of Ivy, long, aggravated strides back and forth. Tears formed in Ivy's eyes. She sniffed.

Jac spoke up. "Trainer, stand down. We need to hear the whole story first."

Kaden didn't sit, but he stopped pacing. He leaned against the wall, arms folded. He appeared casual, but Ivy knew he wasn't.

"Go on, Ivy," ordered Jac.

"I told him I was taking an Uber because I didn't have all day to wait on him. That wasn't the smartest thing to say, but it worked. It seemed like he was going to say something but didn't. He jabbed his hand in his pocket and pulled out a wad of cash mixed with crumpled bits of paper and change. He slammed it down on the hallway table and left. I guess he was trying to be a gentleman and pay for the ride, but I didn't take his money. He had a folded business card and a small drive. I grabbed the card and drive and left the rest.

"I was hurrying down the hall and looked into an open door. It was another office, and Bubba was in there. He saw me as I passed. He called out some crude comment as always. I didn't stop. I was almost in the front game room when I heard a pop. I've grown up around guns my whole life. I knew that was a gunshot. I didn't know if it was JJ or the other man who got shot, but I wasn't waiting around to find out."

The room was quiet except for keys clacking under Sharlee's fingers. Kaden had returned to hold her hands again, and she felt him squeeze them.

"Then you came here," said Monroe.

"Oh, no. I went down the street to a big mall and then called Uber. I was shaking like a leaf, but I figured that it was something important that I just saw and heard. Now I had another bit of importance in my hand. I didn't know what, I still don't, but I know it was significant because before I got my car, JJ was calling me. I drove to my place on the property, and he called the house. Finally, I answered. He was alive, so he must have been the one who did the shooting. He sent me flowers, a huge bouquet, and said how sorry he was that he didn't take me to the auto shop."

"That it?" asked Garrett.

Ivy shook her head. "I said I just had things to take care of now that I had my car back. I thought he was going to insist. Instead, he said he wanted to take me to dinner. I agreed I could go to him the next night after I finished my dance class at 6:00. I shoved what I could in my backpack. I couldn't take much in case he was watching me."

"Why didn't you call me?"

"I kept trying to call you, Kaden. I left four messages and hung up the other times. I had your cell number, but I knew that you might be working. I didn't want to jeopardize you or your job, so I kept calling your office. Now I know why you never answered."

"You can always get to me. I told you to call Sharlee. Plus, Becky and Jessie are always able to answer the phone."

"I felt awkward calling after I had left you. I didn't even know if they'd answer my call."

"Fair enough," said Kaden, "but you're mine, family, and you don't shy away from getting help again, hear me?"

"Yes. Anyway, I drove straight here. When I was almost to your office building, I heard about the explosion earlier that day."

"Good, now that we have that over with, do you need my rubber paddle?"

"Monroe, I think I can handle my girl."

Mark and Carter had left to take care of some business but strode back in the door just as Monroe offered his beloved tool.

Mark laughed. "Only in this group would that not be a suspicious statement, Monroe."

Monroe grinned and shrugged.

Jac spoke impatiently. "Where is the drive now?"

"In Sharlee's box of assorted drives. She went to the bathroom that first night and everyone else was talking about what had happened. I dropped it in the box with the others."

"Hid in plain sight. Good thinking." Jac seemed impressed. "But I agree with Monroe. Kaden needs to heat your ass for you. You put yourself in entirely too much danger. That bullet could have been for you if things had gone a different way. It's clear what happened now."

Carter began to fill in the blanks. "Okay, so JJ thought you might come here to Kaden. He thought, if he could take down the building, it would be difficult to find him, and JJ could get to you first. When that didn't work, he already had you tracked, and he knew where you were likely to hole up. When storming Kaden's condo didn't work, they were able to track you here. While it's well protected, it's not impenetrable."

"That was our midnight callers trying to beat the "A" team at their own game on their own playing field. We schooled them, and now they have to deal with the police. I'm sure it isn't the last we'll hear from them. Obviously, the drive and what she might have seen and heard are more important than Ivy or her out of the way property. The stakes are much higher now."

Mark asked Sharlee, "Can you get into the drive?"

"I will."

"If we could only get it cracked, we'd see what was so important," said Garrett.

Jac asked. "Where is that business card?"

"I don't know. Still in my purse, most likely."

Levi stood up from the wall he was leaning on. He shook his head. "No, Carter and I went over all your things with a fine-toothed comb looking for the tracking device. We didn't run onto a business card."

Garrett stood and walked the perimeter of the room as he reasoned out loud. "Cracking the code is paramount to getting a handle on what they want that we have. And JJ is more likely the leader, not the follower, based on his behavior. The card isn't likely to be as important as the drive."

"But it could contain a clue as to where their business location is, besides Bubba's place."

"I told you the name of the place he owns. Or at least I think he owns. Kingdom Games," said Ivy.

"Okay," said Kaden, "but I don't think JJ would be carrying around Bubba's business card in his pocket. It had to be some other business card with some significance."

"So, I'm screwed."

Jac grinned as though he was having fun. Ivy thought he just might be a little sadistic. "Far from it. But it means this isn't over. We might have to take the battle to their backyard, where they have more to lose. I don't like the fight on my own lawn. Charlotte, you, and Trainer, dive deep and let's see what's on that drive that's so important they would expose themselves and kill people over. Once we have that information, we'll plan, then start blowing some shit up. This week might not be so bad after all." The glee in Jac's expression made the others grin. Boys and their toys came to Ivy's mind.

Levi walked further into the room. "My kind of fun. I fucking love this team."

The men laughed. Ivy didn't because she was sure she had just put Kaden in danger again. Trouble did follow her, even when she didn't expect it. All she wanted was insurance against JJ. Now it sounded like it would be anything but safe for her, Kaden, or any of the others. She didn't want to leave the safety of Kaden, but if she cared about him the way she thought she did, wasn't that the best choice?

Charlotte pulled the drive from the box. "Okay, let's see what we have."

"Maybe I should just take it back. They will leave you all alone." Ivy stood.

Jac shook his head. "And yet, that would not only throw you from the frying pan into the fire, but it also wouldn't satisfy the mob because they are not interested in confirmation on whether or not we know what the drive had on it, they will assume we do and take appropriate action to save whatever operation and information are on here. That's how I would see it if the situation were flipped. So, we have to take countermeasures."

Kaden wrapped her in his arms. "And no, it isn't your fault that we are dealing with this. It is John Jester's and Marciano, Bubba and all the rest. Hell, I'm sorry to say, it is partly your mother's fault unless you think she has no idea about Marciano's business dealings."

Sharlee added. "It is possible, but I'm not sure how likely. Most women want to know what their husband does for a living."

"Oh, not necessarily. If my mom can have her dinner parties, fancy clothes, and afternoons at the country club, life is good. I'm a bit of a disappointment. She has a cook, a housekeeper, two maids, and a driver. She lacks for nothing."

Kaden kissed the top of Ivy's head. "Well, just be careful when speaking with her."

"I have been, but she isn't really interested in me. She hasn't even asked what I've been doing away for so long. I'm not sure she remembers when I left. That's how it's always been. The housekeeper was the person I bounced things off of because she listened."

The group waited to see if Sharlee could read the information she was downloading.

Chapter Eight

K aden leaned close to Ivy. "You good?"
     "Yeah, of course."
     "As I thought, you aren't, but you will be."

He dropped a sizzling kiss on her lips and had to force himself to step back. Ivy would always intoxicate him. As he lifted his head, he made eye contact with Carter and then Mark. Their acknowledgment was a mere whisper of movement, but it was enough for him to know they got his message: she's fragile but feisty. They understood because they had one of their own, making their camaraderie priceless. One last quick kiss and assurance before standing, Jessie and Becky were already making their way to where he was. Good. That would give him the time he needed to find out what was worth starting a war over.

His own feelings aside, he didn't think the mob would have thought Ivy worth the grand gesture of throwing an incendiary device twice. The more he thought about it, the less he thought it was about being sore losers and wanting Ivy and more about getting their information back. Kaden had a plan to get what the team needed while giving the mob back what they thought they wanted without jeopardizing his girl. It was a formulating plan that he liked the longer he thought about it.

IVY ADMIRED KADEN'S confident stride as he headed toward Sharlee and the bank of computer screens. She had resented Sharlee when she first met her in Montana. Obviously, she and Kaden had a close, special relationship, and for a few moments, Ivy thought they were an item. They were so comfortable with each other, but once Jac walked into the room, there was no doubt Sharlee belonged to him. The possessiveness rolled off Jac in waves. Kaden didn't show any of that towards his friend. Protective, yes, possessive, not at all. But he did display those traits with Ivy. She didn't want anyone to doubt she was his and he was hers.

Finding Jac and Sharlee were a couple encouraged Ivy to explore the man that was Kaden Trainer. She had thought at the time that a man was the last thing she would ever need. Besides, he was bossy. That was one of the first things she had noticed about him. Kaden wasn't a quiet man, but he was silent often. His presence spoke loudly enough that his voice was unnecessary.

The annoying man seemed to consider it his personal job to keep her safe. Even more irritating was Ivy found she didn't mind. Later, as they spent more time together after leaving the awful experience of Cramer-Jones, kidnapping and stolen horses in Montana, she found her feelings were growing for Kaden. That was unnerving and frightening. Commitments weren't her thing... until Kaden.

The comfort he brought to her was something she'd never had before. Ivy had no doubt that the man would do what was necessary to keep her happy and safe with his boundaries. Last year, he had introduced her to the men here, except for Levi. He'd joined Kaden's team from one of Jac's other ones after she'd left.

Becky was there, and she had met Jessie a few times with Mark in passing, but really, she didn't know either woman. She'd known Sharlee, but that woman had kept her distance. Jac and Sharlee had had a baby since Ivy had left. Life had changed for both of them. All of them.

Jessie and Mark had gotten married a few months ago. Becky and Carter were dating exclusively now. How did she connect with women who obviously had it all together? These women knew what they wanted, and they didn't sacrifice what they'd wanted for what they thought they needed.

No, that wasn't fair. Ivy did need distance from everything, even Kaden. It was space that she had used to pull her life back together. She'd never wanted to leave, but once Jocelyn O'Connor had broken through some of Ivy's barriers about the whole kidnapping thing and the root causes of her fears, Ivy had felt suffocated.

Ivy needed freedom even from Kaden, whom she thought she'd stay with for a long time, maybe forever. Unfortunately, she hadn't realized at the time that she could have simply gotten her own condo and worked through her life while staying in his.

It was time she'd never get back, but this was good too. What was done was done. She would make such good memories the missed ones would be forgotten. She felt the warmth of Kaden's lips leave hers before he stood and walked away. Looking up at his receding back, she saw the approaching women as Jessie sat on one side of her while Becky took the chair next.

"You ladies don't have to hang out with me. I can go riding."

Becky grimaced. "Please don't. I can't ride."

"Sure, you can," encouraged Ivy.

"Okay, let me phrase it another way. I don't want to learn. Horses aren't my thing."

"You're missing out."

"I'm with Becky on this one. I'm just not a horse person. I mean, I appreciate them and all, but I'm not a dog person either."

"Okay, well, it's how I let off steam and clear my head. What do you do?"

Jessie grinned. "Come on, I'll show you."

In ten minutes, they were walking out of the changing room that came complete with swimsuits and heading for the indoor pool."

"This is incredible. An indoor pool? I haven't gone swimming in a while. I miss it."

"Then let's get in. We both swim," said Becky. "I hate exercise, and while the guys usually use the indoor gym in the next room, I use this. Carter makes me use the gym if I don't get some swimming in at least three times a week, so I try to make sure I don't miss often. Besides, it's fun."

Jessie walked to the edge. "I'm trying to swim as well as Mark. The dumb Marine didn't tell me he was on some special team or other until I set that as my goal a year ago. Now I have to do it because I won't back down."

"I would never try to go against Kaden physically, even with his messed-up elbow, but I do okay."

"Because you have all of that martial arts training which, by the way, Jac requires self-defense for every employee. At first, it drove me crazy. I'm not aggressive, you know, but after working with these guys for a while, I get it." Becky swam away to start laps.

Jessie came back to Ivy. "Come swim laps with us."

"Okay, but I want to ask you something. Are these guys always intense one minute and laid back the next?"

"Yep. They can drop stress in two-point three seconds. Amazing really. Now not Sharlee but the guys, yeah. Come on."

The women started swimming together, but soon, each found her own stroke rhythm and then just continued on independent of the others but still swimming laps. It had been a while since Ivy had done so many laps. When she stopped, too exhausted to go further, the other women had left the pool. She vaguely remembered telling them she would be in soon. How long had that been? Time to get out.

Ivy waited a few minutes as she gave herself a little stabilization time. She climbed out of the pool and sat on the side, not daring to take a real step until she had gotten used to gravity again. She felt heavy and sluggish. As she finished the climb out of the pool, her legs buckled, and she felt light-headed. Thinking she was going to hit the ceramic flooring and cringing at the thought of the pain but not able to devise a way to stop the inevitable, strong, firm hands grabbed both arms and supported her to the bench.

"Dammit, Ivy, you were in there too long."

"No, I wasn't, really." A wave of nausea passed over her, and then it was gone. Her head stabilized. If she could only walk more steadily.

"I watched you leave, and the other two have been done fifteen minutes at least. You've been swimming laps for a long time. The ladies sounded the alarm when you didn't follow them out."

"I had no idea. I just got into a zone and kept going."

"Let's get you in the showers." His hold had grown gentler, and his voice lost its hardness.

"You aren't angry, are you?"

"No. But I'm monitoring you next time. I know what it's like when you need stress relief and use exercise to find it. You need a spotter."

"I'm not a child."

"No, ma'am, you aren't, but I'm spanking that ass later."

"You are not."

"Yep, safety. If I weren't coming to get you, you would have fallen with no one to help until we found you on the cameras. Hitting your head on this flooring could kill you. Oh, yes, I'm spanking you because you're old enough to know better."

Ivy tried to yank her arm away from him, and Kaden let go. "I'm fine. See?"

"I can do it now if you like, but the flat of my hand on your wet butt cheeks might not be the best choice. Just saying."

"I'm going to take a quick shower and get my clothes on."

"Need help?"

"No. I'll come to find you when I'm done."

Kaden chuckled. "Nice try. I'll get you a juice and wait for you."

When Ivy opened her mouth to remind him she didn't drink juice, the quirked eyebrow, and his look of no-nonsense changed her mind about challenging him. She turned and peeled off the swimwear and threw it in the hamper.

She entertained the idea of playing the repentant little woman but almost laughed in disgust at the thought. Besides, she wasn't that good of an actress, and Kaden wasn't that gullible. No, she'd just wait until tonight, and if he still wanted to swat her butt, she would reason with him like any other person.

Except Kaden wasn't any other person, he was the man she was falling back in love with and this time, she didn't carry a world of baggage. She did bring him trouble and suddenly, as she sluiced water over her body, wondered what the others might think about her. Whenever she was around, there was trouble. At least something they had to deal with before things settled down.

That was a sobering realization. Ivy finished rinsing off and got out. Kaden wrapped her in a towel and began to dry her hair with a second towel. It was a little awkward until Kaden spoke. They both wanted him to continue. She thought it was asking too much.

"Let me take care of you, Ivy. You steal my pleasure when you fight me on doing things for you."

"O-okay."

The awkwardness faded away as he systematically rubbed her dry, running the towel over her wet body with brisk, careful strokes. When he finished, she redressed and was handed a bottle of juice.

"Kaden, there are too many calories in juice. I'll drink water."

"Okay, I'll drink it. You drink vitamin water with electrolytes."

Ivy wrinkled her nose. "Why not just water?"

"Are you really asking me that?"

"No, I guess not. I know why. It's just that I don't want to get used to this. Soon we'll go back to a normal existence after we leave here, right?"

Kaden stared at her for a moment and then smiled as he reached in the fridge to grab another drink, opening it and handing the bottle to her. His free arm wrapped around her as she threw the towels in the hamper.

"Sweetheart, you do understand that I'm not in the military any longer, right? The work I do now I get well compensated for doing. What I'm telling you is none of us is hurting for money. If I want to buy a new car, I take on a few extra jobs in a month, and I've financed a new car. Well, in theory. My rigs are pricier than that."

"Oh, well, then I don't understand why Jac needs all of this if it isn't to supplement the teams and his business."

"You mean, why does Jac have this when the rest of us don't? Partly because it's him and Sharlee in his family home, both with high incomes. There's baby Storm to protect, and it takes people to help support the domestic side of things to make it all work. Plus, Jac has two racehorses that he owns and races for a hobby. I'm from Maine, and my parents still live in the home they built forty-some years ago. My tastes are similar to theirs, simpler. We just have different backgrounds and different goals."

"Are you going to want to go to Maine when you're done working?"

"Good question. I don't think so. My family is here, and my parents are in Maine. I visit, but I like Kentucky, and I'm part of these people now. So are you now if you want to be. It will begin to feel more like home after we finish with this mob issue. So, I do live like this at home, especially in the last year since you've been gone. We'll figure it all out."

"As nice as it is, I can't live in your condo forever."

"We won't. I'm considering a more permanent place after we've gotten used to living together again. Mark did when he wanted to bring in Jessie. Come on. We're having dinner soon, then we'll discuss what has been uncovered on the flash drive."

"Kaden, I worry I've brought too much trouble with me, but I'm afraid to go it alone now that I know how dangerous everyone really is."

"Beginning to sound like a broken record, Ivy. We can handle the disruption, and I think it might buy us some points with the feds once we figure out what we have. And I want you to be scared enough to do what I tell you but not too intimidated to settle into life. Organized crime is here for good, but we can fix things enough to live a normal, healthy life."

"I'm going to hold you to that."

"I'm good with that."

Kaden took Ivy's bottle and threw it away with his as they entered the kitchen. "What smells so good?"

"Pot roast. I'm serving in fifteen minutes."

"Can I set the table?" offered Ivy.

The Reynaud's cook, in his second generation of employment, shook his head. "No, already done, but you can take in these dishes to go with the main meal and put them on the sideboard. Thank you."

The bowls of salad and vegetables were placed in the dining room, alongside the beverages and ice. Ivy went upstairs to comb her hair, and when she came back down, she heard Mark and Jac talking. She stopped and listened to see if she should just go down or wait until they were done. She should have just gone down. What she heard by waiting ruined her appetite.

"Jac, are you sure she couldn't have known about the contents of that drive?"

"Not sure how she could have gotten into it. It took Sharlee and Kaden a little trial and error before they found the key to unlock the encryption. There were two passwords as well."

"Okay, so not actually gotten into the drive itself, but it's possible she knew what was on it, and that's why she kept it. She's smart enough to keep something she knows is that important to the Marciano Family. She already told us that it was for insurance."

"No, I don't believe so. Sharlee monitored her heart rate when we showed her photos connected to Marciano and the intruders last night. She didn't show any subterfuge. I believe her."

"Please don't feel harsh of me if I reserve my judgment for a little while longer. I hope you're right, though, because Kaden is in deep with her. He certainly acts like a man falling fast."

Jac chuckled. "It happens to the best of us. It will be good for him to join the ranks of the demoted devoted."

"Hey, speak for yourself. I prefer the orgasmic operative."

"Yeah, say that in mixed company. Sharlee already has me using phonetics for much less offensive language. She's likely to come after you with a butcher knife and take care of that problem."

"Shit. I don't think you're joking. That woman scares me sometimes." Both men laughed as they walked away to join the others for dinner.

Jac seemed to believe she had nothing to do with the mess she was in, or at least not on purpose, but Mark, the one that always seemed so dark and brooding, had some grave doubts. She didn't know how to convince him otherwise. She needed to clear her head, and it was a damn shame because she was hungry after that swim. She wouldn't starve if she missed a meal, but Kaden would have a fit. She tried to convince herself that she'd be fine, but her stomach and her butt were waging an argument against that school of thought.

Racing back to grab her light jacket, the only one she'd brought, she prayed the night wasn't too cold. As she was slipping out the side door closest to the stables, Ivy had no doubt that it would take a simple check of the cameras to know that someone had left and by what door. This place was probably equipped with heat emissions. Racing to the stables, she found them empty at this time of night. It was dinner for everyone, it seemed.

No time for a saddle, Ivy prayed a bridle was enough. Her muscles were a little sore, but not much. Her left foot normally had a stirrup to put her foot in for leverage, but she used the stall railing and heaved up, throwing her right leg high and over to slide the rest of her body on. Holding the mane and reins, she wheeled the beautiful quarter horse named Windsong around and encouraged him out the stable side exit.

Ivy was happy she had ridden this beauty every day since she and Jac had taken him out the first day. She had learned the main trail and would stay on it. She would never risk the horse's life, but she absolutely loved the freedom this handsome ride gave her. She wasn't out but for a few moments when floodlights came on. They didn't blind her, but they startled her and her mount.

"Whoa, boy. It's okay."

Ivy crooned and rubbed her hand on his neck until he quit dancing and resumed walking. She half expected the guys to come out in force or Monroe to wield his famous rubber paddle, but no one came. She knew someone was watching her, but she didn't care. Only when she decided she could go back did she worry what Kaden would say.

Ivy wanted to be with him, but sometimes it was difficult. They had little free time together, and while it was a huge house, they weren't alone. She never seemed to forget that except for the bedroom they were in, they showed up on security cameras everywhere. She arrived back at the stables and set about taking care of Windsong. Even that was therapeutic. Long strokes of the brush and listening to him munch his extra alfalfa made her happy.

She hummed and cooed as she worked. After shutting the gate and putting away the supplies, she washed her hands. Warm arms encircled her waist, and she instinctively stiffened. Then as the familiarity of the man behind her, with his particular earthy scent combined with his normal deodorant, settled around her, she continued to dry her hands. There was no doubt it was Kaden. He leaned into her as she relaxed against him.

"Feel better?"

"Yes. No. I think I should just go."

Silence met her statement. "Is that what you want to do?"

"It's what would end all of this mess."

"Are you responsible for the mess?"

"Of course not. Well, I am responsible for bringing it here, Kaden. I know your friend Mark thinks I am part of the whole Marciano family. That I set this up or something, but you know I didn't, right?"

"Listen, he's your friend too. He was extra cautious. With you listening in to the conversation, he threw out some bait to see if you would bite."

"And I did."

"No. You got upset and went to clear your head. You didn't take off or call someone to meet you. That would have been hard to explain but going for a ride and leaving your cell phone inside, which we will talk about later, by the way, is understandable."

"He tried to set me up? What an asshole."

"The thing is, he was protecting his wife and the other women as well as everyone else."

"But he had to doubt me, or he wouldn't have needed to test me."

"Good point," said a voice from the entrance. Ivy stiffened in Kaden's arms.

"You."

"Me." Mark took a step closer. "I think Trainer did a good job of explaining my reasoning, but I think you need more."

"I don't need anything from you. If you wanted me to leave, the less shitty thing to do would have been to tell me."

"True, but then I wouldn't have gotten the indisputable truth. I didn't want you to leave. Ivy, I was protecting my family, of which you have very recently become a part of, and if this guy next to you is right, a permanent part."

"I don't have a brother, but if I did and he did something like that to me, I don't know if he would be able to sleep at night."

"Oh, sweetheart, I *am* your brother now, and if you tried to sneak in my room, I would take you down and then scorch your ass."

"Whatever. I don't know how long it's going to take to forgive you."

"Take your time, sweetheart, but Ivy, don't ever doubt that I'm on your side no matter what. You need something, and Kaden isn't close by, you call me. You have a family that excels in taking care of problems, but if you don't call us and we find out, you know how we deal with safety issues."

"Oh, but I thought..." She turned to Kaden.

Her lover nodded. "He's right. You call the nearest person if you can't get to me fast enough. Promise me."

"I'm not going to promise that."

"Yes, you are. The team's numbers are programmed into your phone by initials. You will call me or whoever can get to you quickest. Promise."

Mark took another step closer. "You have a stubborn woman, Kaden. You haven't paddled her ass enough. There's leather all around us. Just saying. It works wonders on mine."

"What?" Ivy hated she had a warm flushed feeling at the thought of leather and her stern, chastising Kaden.

"Promise, Ivy." Mark was pressuring her.

"Promise, sweetheart or turn around." Kaden was serious.

"Okay, okay. I promise."

Mark nodded. "Good. Now, finish up out here. You have dinner in the oven. We have a meeting to finish, and then we start moving into our new digs. Jac just secured them tonight. He's stoked, and we won't be able to go home until he has told us everything. He's anal about shit like that."

"When are we going home, Kaden?"

"We need to talk about it later tonight, okay?"

"See you back inside. Oh, and Trainer, your woman has a sassy mouth. You might want to take care of that."

"Not funny," Ivy called after Mark.

"Not kidding," he answered. "Squirt."

"He's right about one thing, you have more than earned a hot ass. I'd rather do it here before we go back in. Turn around, and before you say it, any sass will get you bared. Believe me, Ivy."

She stomped her foot and grunted but turned around and allowed Kaden to lean her over the tack table. This was the worst part, the anticipation. She felt her heartbeat increase and her core lubricate. He grabbed one of the strips of leather left there and wrapped the excess around his hand like a belt. It was wide and would cover her ass with a couple of strikes.

"This is for swimming too long, for keeping secrets, and for taking off tonight without letting me know where you were going."

"Kaden, I—"

"Have the need to strip, honey?"

"No!" Ivy went silent.

"You will learn to talk to me, share with me, and not hide important things that can harm you or others. Safety first. No excuses will ever be accepted. And I don't care about your sassy mouth, but I'll throw that in because it was a bit caustic tonight."

His foot kicked her legs apart like an officer might do when he was frisking someone. "Give me your hands. You know the drill. It hasn't been that long."

Kaden laid down the leather over her jeans covered bottom with sincere intent. Ivy wondered if he would have been kinder if she had been bare. No, not worth the chance. The burn was building, and before Ivy realized it, she possessed a flaming ass and was grunting and squealing with every application of leather. She stomped her feet.

"Kaden," she gasped, "I can't take any more."

"You can, but it's been a while since your behavior was regularly addressed. I'll cut you some slack for a while." The leather landed back on the table, and he turned Ivy around in his arms. He kissed her lips salty with her tears. She shed more.

"I'm sorry."

"I know. It's over. Let's go get your dinner and find out about our new place of business. I'm curious about what Jac bought and to see how far Sharlee's decoding program has gotten. What Mark said, he meant. I want you to know that. And he spoke for everyone. They all feel the same."

"Sure, after you told him to come out here."

"I didn't. I was pissed at him, at Jac for going along with it, and with you for taking off."

"Thank you for caring about me. Why was I the only one who got the strap?"

Kaden smiled. "Honey, I'm falling in love with you. I think I have loved you ever since I first set eyes on you in Montana, but now, I know it's going deeper. Please don't go anywhere without letting me know or someone here. I couldn't bear it if I had to find you again. The next time might not have a happy ending."

"I won't. I can't seem to leave because even though I want to be a hero and take the evil from your door, I can't. I want you too much. I want us."

"Thank God."

Chapter Nine

The room was full of chatter. "Hey, what'd we miss?"

"Kaden, I think we're close to cracking the code. Come and see what we have so far."

Jessie waved Ivy over to stand with her in front of Sharlee's screen, looking at what appeared to be a medium-sized concrete gray and white building with a circular drive and a few parking spaces. The next photo showed the back of the building where a small parking lot sat.

"Is this it? The new office? It looks, um, industrial and unremarkable."

"It's perfect, right?" Becky left Carter's side as Jac got closer to the photo display of the interior and exterior.

"I guess."

"It is," said Jac. "We aren't selling cosmetics. We're a security company."

Ivy nodded. "True."

Jac continued enthusiastically. "It's one of those flex buildings. The kind that allows us to retrofit what we need without too much hassle. It'll take a few weeks to get it all set up, but we get in tomorrow morning when they record the deed."

"This is the interior of the building. I'm working on doing a government swap. They come in and help me outfit the place, and I take one contract with them, free of charge. I think we got a deal. Now with the additional threat coming into our backyard, very literally, we need this to be a small fortress but look like a normal set of offices."

"Are we setting our reception out front again because I might have something to say about that," said Carter.

Becky sighed as though this was an old conversation. "Honey, I've been fine."

"So far, but we own this building, so we have the opportunity to make the configuration the way that works best for us." Carter was warming to his subject.

"No, Carter's right," said Garrett. "That was the whole reasoning behind deciding to move anyway. Then the little explosion made it necessary to move. But I say we sit down and start drawing out the floor plan. I think we can easily put a receptionist behind a sheet of ammo proof glass."

"That's what I'm talking about," said Carter.

"But not Becky," said Jac. "She's going to be in my outer office because she's my assistant and because I didn't want any grief from you, Carter."

"Good thinking," said Carter.

"It comes with a basement," added Monroe. "I can think of lots of fun things to use that for."

Jac grinned. "Storage, training, settling mouthy women."

"Hey," Sharlee said from the other side of the room, "I heard that."

"There went the surprise," said Jac.

Jac was in a good mood, and Ivy knew he would have this set up in no time. She was reminded many times this week that when Jac put his mind to dealing with a problem, he became like a steamroller. There was no stopping his forward momentum. A person moved out of the way or got flattened.

"If you want to draw up your plans by hand, I can formalize them and do calculations on my Architectural CAD programs according to what you need. You'll have something professional to give your architect or contractor. It takes a few hours to get the basics down but then the calculations are factored in automatically. That is if it would help you," offered Ivy.

Kaden walked over and sat next to Ivy. "I didn't know you could do that, honey."

"It was my minor. Well, computer graphic design was, and one of my instructors was an architect. She said it might come in handy sometime, so she taught us this CAD program. I had thought to be an architect, but after getting my undergrad and grad, I was tired. I stuck with graphics as a hobby. I decided to finish my education class by class after I finished my degrees."

"Because..." asked Monroe.

"I like to make my own schedule. And it relaxes me to create story games and the graphics for them."

"How long did you go to college?" asked Kaden.

"Oh, I went for five years. I'm good at it, Jac, and it's profitable, too. So, you interested?"

"Hell yeah. Everyone, get your section planned and bring them with you. Here's the address on this page. Looks like Charlotte's program is still working, so let's get this done so we can spread out again. Kaden, see what you can do to help Charlotte. Ladies, I defer to your interior design know-how and guys, we have a security grid to design."

After everyone but Kaden and Ivy was gone, Jac hugged Ivy and sat down next to Sharlee. Jac spoke; his voice showed his sincerity. "Thank you for trusting us and letting us in on your skillset. You have to know we are going to use you now that we know you have those abilities. Graphics is useful, but Psychology? When you get that Ph.D., you will be a hot commodity. I would never have figured you for something that heavy."

"Because I'm a blonde?"

"Young."

"I have a feeling you already knew what skills I had."

"True," he said ruefully. "Charlotte got it all on the day you came back, but I wasn't going to bring it up unless you did. You know I've already come up with uses. I'll pay you for your time when you do jobs for us, just like a contractor. Charlotte won't have to do some of the work she has been doing, and that will free her up for other work that is equally time-consuming and use a different set of skills."

"That's not necessary." Jac looked stymied. "Paying me. I've been staying at your home."

Jac looked at Kaden. "I bet Kaden will want you to get paid for working. Besides, the team can crash here anytime. And, when you get that final degree? I'd be a fool not to box you in with some kind of contract."

Kaden nodded. "If it takes some real time, I agree you should get paid, Ivy. You can help people out, but what Jac is talking about is when we have graphics or design work, or even some profiling, or anything in that area of expertise. It's easier if he can pay you for the work, then he won't feel bad about asking. And I can think of some ways we could adapt your gaming to create strategy war games for practice. That would be a contract job, and he will pay you."

"But I don't like regular hours."

"Good, because there won't always be work, but when there is, and you can do it, then if you agree, I'll send it your way."

"I'll have to pick up my system from home then. Besides, you'll need a forensic psychologist for profiling."

"We'll get there, and so will you. Right now, let's work on the office building."

"I, um, sure. That will work."

Jac leaned back in the sofa cushion and drew Charlotte into his side. He crossed his legs in a sign of relaxation. "Good. Next, I wanted to apologize about tonight with Mark. It was a cruel thing to do. While I didn't have any qualms, Mark wanted to be sure. Then he felt bad. You should have busted his balls for that stunt."

"She did. Mark also told her she was family now and there are rules and responsibilities associated with that, like calling when she needs help."

Jac nodded. Ivy sat up further in her seat.

"You people are full of rules."

"And responsibilities. I take mine very seriously. Ask Charlotte."

Charlotte nodded. "He's right. Jac takes care of his own but what he always asks is that they don't put themselves, especially the women, in unnecessary danger."

Kaden laughed. "Yes, like driving to a place on a map after hours without telling anyone and then finding themselves stranded. And instead of calling one of us for help, she calls a damn tow truck."

Sharlee smiled. "Okay, fine, but I was just learning you guys. Ivy, you will likely make some dumb mistakes you didn't realize weren't allowed any longer either, simply because they are over-protective baboons. Sometimes the rules are messed up, but they are lovely baboons."

"And sometimes," added Jac, "they could save your life."

Sharlee sat forward. "Which brings me to the Keep Safe program that I created. You need to learn how to use it in case you ever need it."

"I'll think about it."

Jac spoke casually, but Ivy knew he was serious. "Think hard. I'd hate for Kaden to have to inject a subcutaneous tracking device in you, but we will if we have to."

"Okay fine. I'll learn it."

Sharlee smiled. "Tomorrow afternoon, before you go back to the condo."

"I hadn't told her yet, Charlotte. You do know you talk too much, right?"

"Oh, shut up, Kaden. If you'd tell her things, she wouldn't have to hear them from me."

"Did I hear Mark call you 'Squirt?'" Jac cut off the building banter.

"Yes, but he won't be doing it again."

"I like it, and the guys will jump on it quickly if you don't tell them you don't like it. It's how Sharlee got her nickname."

Ivy stifled a yawn. "I'll tell them tomorrow."

"We need to go to bed. I'm beat," said Kaden.

"Okay, us too. Are we good, Ivy?" Jac's eyebrow lifted in query.

She nodded. "Yes, we're good."

"Back to one big happy family. Just the way I like it, but we have to get operations out of my house. I don't like that."

They were going back to the condo tomorrow. Ivy couldn't help but suppress a shiver of anticipation.

THE NEXT MORNING WAS spent at the new building, and Ivy worked on getting the plan drafted. The rest had other work to get done, and after talking through a few revisions to make the flow of the building work, Ivy was done by dinner.

During the same time that Ivy was drafting, Kaden and Sharlee worked on unlocking the codes. The information extraction went fast once Sharlee got past the second password. The encryption took a little longer but finally, around dinner, it was completely decoded.

The bulk of the teams had gone to handle security jobs they had already scheduled. It left only Jac and Sharlee, Kaden, and Ivy for dinner.

Kaden put his silverware down. "Are you ready to go home?"

"Really? No offense, but I'm so ready. But is it safe? I mean..."

"I think so. I've had the place on camera, and we haven't had any visitors. I've beefed up the personal security, and we have agreed that if the safe house is open, we will go there next time."

"Next time?" Ivy could feel her concern rise exponentially.

"Bad choice of words. Should you feel unsafe, we will go there to alleviate your fears."

"I'm not a kid afraid of the dark, Kaden. I am afraid already. Maybe I should just go to a hotel or something, so you aren't put in danger. JJ won't find me."

Sharlee gave her a warning shake of her head, but Ivy saw it too late. "We do need to go home because I can see there are some home truths I haven't addressed well enough. The first of which is if you mention danger and leaving in the same conversation again or leaving at all, you will be on a retraining regimen I had hoped we could avoid. I won't tell you again. The danger is here until we eradicate it no matter what you do, and you leaving is not a subject I'm willing to discuss right now or ever."

"When do we leave because I have a few things to discuss with you, too," said Ivy."

Ivy didn't know what exactly, but she didn't want to be the only one without some control. Kaden's grin and a shake of his head told her he was enjoying this exchange.

"I'm having dessert first. Then we can go."

"Perfect. I hope my car is still there." When Kaden didn't say anything, she pressed the point. "My car Kaden. I know you had yours brought here, but what about mine?"

"Still there."

"Good. I'll need it tomorrow."

Ivy intercepted the look that Jac and Kaden exchanged but decided this wasn't the place to have an argument. There would be time for clearing the air later. Kaden didn't respond, which was a good idea. After thanking Jac and Sharlee for their generosity, she went upstairs to gather her few things and was in the foyer before Kaden was done with dessert.

She walked into the den and saw what must have been the code all over Sharlee's screens. On one screen, she kept seeing the word Carp and Son, as a business name in several places. Where had she seen that name before? Ivy tried to remember, but she couldn't. It was one of those annoying 'not quite' memories. It would bug her until they figured it out.

Sharlee walked into the room. "It took a while, but we finally cracked the encryption. Trouble is, it still doesn't make enough sense to tell us much."

"I recognize this Carp and Son, but I can't remember from where. It isn't quite right, but I don't know why. I've seen this not that long ago, I do know that. Maybe one of my students works for them, or possibly I passed it on my way here. I don't know."

"Well, I haven't done much deep diving on this yet, but let me pull up the name like a company and see if it gives us anything."

After a few minutes, all they could find was a car disposal place. "A junkyard."

Sharlee shook her head. "Yes and no. I think that this is where they take totaled cars and part them out before crushing them."

"I don't know any place like that." After they pulled it up on a locator map, neither women recognized the business or that part of town. "I've never been there."

"We'll work on it." Sharlee turned to look at the code again.

Ivy cocked her head. "There must be some significance that we should be aware of, or it wouldn't have been mentioned so often. Maybe that is their meeting place."

Jac walked in behind them. "I thought that was what they did at Bubba's pseudo-palace."

Sharlee asked. "This place that you got the Uber from, was it in this part of town?"

"No, on the edge of the industrial district. Seemed odd for a gamers' place, but I guess no one cared so long as they weren't bothered. I called the Uber from the strip mall next door."

"Show me." They worked a little longer, and then Kaden walked in, putting a stop to any more work.

"I'll help you work on that tomorrow. Tonight, I need to get my girl home."

"It will be nice to only worry about one set of lungs waking Storm up in the night," said Jac dryly.

Ivy could feel her face burn with mortification. Sharlee lit into her husband about his lack of filter. Ivy appreciated the woman coming to her rescue, but she just wanted to leave the den and her embarrassment behind. Jac winked at Ivy as she passed him, Sharlee still complaining in the background. Ivy couldn't help but smile and feel better.

Jac waved. "Have a good night."

Kaden kissed her temple and led her toward the front door. "Night," he said.

Once they arrived at the condo, Ivy was shown the more extensive security system as they walked in the front door.

"There is a camera at the front door facing the hallway and elevator, but we aren't notified of its use, or we'd go crazy. There is a camera at the elevators in the hall. We've upgraded the door and inside cameras. The intercom system is smart, so all I have to do is say *tell Ivy I'm home* or whatever, and the system is linked to every room."

"Sounds a bit overwhelming."

Kaden stopped and turned around. "I know, and I'm sorry. We'll work on learning things as we go. Tonight, why don't you take a shower and get ready for bed. I had the ladies buy you a few more things. Tomorrow you can order what you want, and we'll go pick it up. I don't want you out right now. Not until we're sure you have nothing to worry about."

"Thanks. I'll order from one of the places I shop. They will have my measurements and deliver."

"Okay, tomorrow. Why don't you go shower?"

Ivy was tired, and a hot shower and crawling between cool sheets sounded amazing. Tomorrow would be a full day of the expected and likely the unexpected, too. She didn't want to think about it until she had to, and tomorrow would be here much too quickly.

After Ivy was asleep, Kaden lay in bed, holding her in his arms. Finally, they were home. It wasn't how he would have liked it, but he did think that it was well on its way to being business as usual.

The code concerned him, and the fact that Ivy was still in danger ate at him. They weren't on their game because they didn't have all of their tools and toys on hand. Jac had gotten the insurance company to replace them, and they were trickling in slowly, but it was too slow for Kaden.

Kaden hadn't ever been an impatient man, but where Ivy was concerned, he wanted things taken care of yesterday and found himself grumpy when it wasn't. He had discussed his hope to look for a more permanent place when all of this mess was over, and things were more settled. Ivy had been less than enthusiastic. Kaden wondered if she was just tired or also disillusioned because either would have made sense.

Looking at the angel he loved, coming back home, and remembering the things they had done together a year ago, Kaden wanted this time to be more realistic. They had visited places, gone out to eat most nights, and looked for outside entertainment. This time it needed to be more of normal life, something they could settle into comfortably. Which was even more reason to get this done quickly and fall into a more natural routine.

Chapter Ten

The business card was lying, folded, on the inside of the closet door. Kaden picked it up, hoping it was a clue to follow about who had been in his home that night a week ago. Carpinelli and Sons, Auctioneers, was written on the card, and his heart pounded a little faster. Ivy must have dropped it as they were exiting through here.

Securing the escape passage and putting his key and flashlight back in their designated spots, Kaden brought the card out into the bedroom and stood in the light. It had a small memory chip, like a cell phone or camera, taped to it. The trespassers didn't find the room, so they didn't find the card. That meant they were ahead of them now.

Kaden thought back and remembered Ivy struggling with her bag for a few seconds as they rushed through the door in the dark. Once he had the flashlight on, they oriented and started out of the building. That must have been when it fell.

Carpinelli and Sons Auctioneers. Something was off about this. He listened to Ivy in the shower to verify she was still busy before pulling out his cell and punching in an access code. He didn't want to worry her more than she was already.

"Sharlee, I have the business card I think we were looking for, and it holds a surprise."

The car crush business they had thought the code was imprinting wasn't Carp and Son but Carpinelli and Sons Auctioneers. They looked up the wrong place. When they looked the right business name up, it was not the same company. It wasn't listed, and that made things sound so much better. They called Levi and Garrett in off their surveillance. No need to waste their time there any longer. No, they would find out where this place was or what it represented. Sharlee would have to do what she did best. Dive deep.

Kaden lowered his voice. "I'm not going to leave her alone even though I have two bodyguards in my front room and enhanced security. When this shit is over, I'm moving us out to a place that I can build security to the level I want. Jac has the right idea. Our own building, our own operation, our own protection."

Sharlee was pounding keys as she talked. "Okay, Kaden, I get it. Maybe there is someplace not too far but not right next door. I'll start working on it after we get through this mess. Now the Feds want to know what is going on with this Marciano family. They found some leads to shipments but were unable to follow up. They say it has the markings of Carlton Marciano. That is our job. Find the info and share it with them. I think we now have everything we need if we could only get the key to reading it all."

Kaden walked further away from the bathroom. "I'll throw this chip into my reader and see if I can understand what it is and how it's important. I think I can remember the coding to unlock the script if it is encrypted. I'll call you back."

"Wait, Kaden, how's Ivy today?" Sharlee said hurriedly.

"I'm worried at how vulnerable all of this makes her. She's at the center of this vortex, and it scares the shit out of me. I haven't told her yet that the Marciano family wants her for what she has and what she might know so much that she has a bounty on her. I almost wish Jac had let that bit of information fly himself. How can I keep her safe until this clusterfuck is over? I'm worried I can't."

"You're not alone. You know that, right? Don't forget the rest of us, but you have to tell her. Coming from the woman's angle here, we need to know everything you can safely tell us. We can help ourselves to stay safe, but not if we don't know the whole story." Sharlee changed directions. "Okay, so we work more efficiently. I'll start creating dossiers on the main members while you work on unraveling the mystery you have. Keep her inside and safe. Have her clothes delivered and not to you?"

"We had already decided to call in the order, but I didn't think about not having it delivered to us here. It could be a beacon that she is here in the building."

"Especially if they have been paying attention and saw you go home last night."

"Shit, this is why we use a team. Okay. Where do I have it delivered?"

"I'll send my shopper to go pick the order up and bring it here with my groceries. It will look like a normal delivery that I have every week. I'll have someone take it over later today."

"Sounds good. Damn, I should put Ivy in your dolled up safe house," said Kaden.

"It isn't that bad. And stop referring to it as my safe house. I was held there against my will."

Kaden laughed. "But not against Jac's. We do what we have to do to keep our women safe. Okay, gotta go. I'll try to unlock this as soon as possible."

Ivy overheard the end of Kaden's conversation that must have been with Sharlee. They were very good friends, and Ivy was jealous of their familiarity and closeness sometimes. Sharlee loved her husband, and Ivy didn't worry that she and Kaden held any deeper affection for the other outside of a friendship. But she wanted that closeness that made you comfortable enough to be painfully honest and daringly teasing.

Ivy believed the emotions that Kaden showed and expressed were real concerning their relationship. And yet, she still felt a distrust, a stiffness in their connection that made her sad. She knew Kaden would want to talk about it. He was the one with the communication mandate when it came to them, but now wasn't the right time to show her vulnerabilities; it was a time to suck it up. So, she did.

"I thought I'd order my clothes. Oh, you found the business card. Where was it?"

"In the back exit."

"Good. So, are you going over to Sharlee's to work on things?"

"Nope. Not leaving you until we don't have anything to worry about."

"That won't work. You have a job to do."

"Feds just asked us to help them on this very thing, so I am working. And don't have your clothes sent to the condo. It might alert anyone watching that you are here. It's a long shot, but we don't want to give anyone a whiff of the possibility of finding you. As far as Marciano knows, you are still at Jac's."

"Unless he saw us leave."

"Yep, unless that happened. Ivy, I didn't want to tell you, but Sharlee insisted. We have intercepted a modified hit out on you. Technically, it says it will pay more for you alive, but will take you dead."

Ivy sat in Kaden's lap. "Now what?"

"We continue to do what we do, but it might have upped the ante. The safe house is looking better and better. Jac is working on that."

"Okay, so where do I send the clothes?" asked Ivy.

"Sharlee's shopper is picking it up for you. Just tell me where you're getting your things from, and the shopper will pick up the order in her errands. She'll drop it off at Sharlee's in her normal delivery, and one of the guys will bring it over."

"Seems like a lot of work for just a little bit of clothes."

"Worth it, though."

"I can wait," decreed Ivy.

"Baby, don't wait. We are just taking extra precautions. It's what we do. Order the clothes."

"Okay, can I see what is on the memory chip?"

"Yep. Here goes."

"Huh, places and times, but no dates. That isn't helpful," said Ivy.

"No, it is." Kaden had Sharlee up on video conference in a few moments. "Sharlee, we've got it. Now go back to where you see the words, Carp and Son, at the beginning. See those numbers? They have two number places, dot, two number places. If we assume the year is this year, I think those are dates, and I have times and places in a list here."

"Got it. So, when it says Carp and Son, it means Carpinelli and Sons Auctioneers. I add in the place and time to the date I have going in order, and we should be golden. I'll have all I need to know to do a drop-off or pick up. Perfect. Now we need to determine if the second number is the month or the day on this read-out."

"Compare it to the Feds intel. A shipment was intercepted, so maybe we can cross-reference to a notation if we have the identifiers. Then we will have the verification we need to go ahead with matching things up. What they were delivering or picking up was anyone's guess, but there was a whole list of things that were lucrative and illegal that Marciano's family was thought to dabble."

Kaden kissed Ivy as she stood, still with a towel around her.

"The next issue is, do we assign names to the initials, or do we just let the Feds do that?"

"No. Unfortunately, this is their one contracted freebie for helping us with acquiring and installing the same state-of-the-art system that they use. So, we will have to at least put our ideas as to who the initials belong to."

"Okay, then let's look at the initials we have. J is for Jester. The infamous JJ," said Kaden.

"Yes, and B we can assume is Bubba. Not sure who C and S are. Does Marciano have a son?"

"Let's see if Ivy knows." Kaden brought Ivy back onto his knee. "Does Marciano have a son?"

"Only one living son. I think my mom said his name is Carlo. But he has a nephew he thinks highly of named Stephan."

"Did you get that? I'm fairly sure those are the two other initials. The rest, well, the Feds will have to do something to earn their pay."

Sharlee read, "Okay, the first entry is J 06.01 will be going fishing with Carp and Son."

"Then I add what I have on my first line: Greenline Wharf 1415. So Greenline Wharf on Jan. 6th at 1415 and JJ is heading up the pick-up or delivery," said Kaden.

They needed to check on things and figure out the two dates that had already come and gone. If they could see a pattern, or something that indicated drop shipments or something else, they could turn it all over to the Feds. The sooner they got Marciano chasing his own tail, the better.

Sharlee continued. "If this matches the one shipment stumbled on by governmental agents, then we're golden. In the meantime, I'm sure the first two numbers represent the day and the second two numbers the month because I have numbers too high to be months first." Sharlee sounded tired.

"You don't sound as though you've gotten much sleep," said Ivy, after Sharlee yawned.

"Shows, I guess. No, I haven't, but I will as soon as this is verified by someone other than us. I'll show Jac, and he can share. I'm going to try to get a nap in. Talk later, and don't go anywhere Ivy. Text me the information on your clothing store. I'll have it delivered this afternoon sometime."

"Thank you for going to all the trouble."

"You're one of us now, so no thanks needed, but you're welcome."

Sharlee signed off. As Kaden finished what he was doing, Ivy wandered around his office. Some of the certificates and photos were new. She picked up what looked like a photo of his team. The military one that no longer existed. She searched each face, knowing they were all taken from this earth while fighting for her freedoms. As she glanced at the last face, she stopped.

"Kaden, that's him. That's Marciano's nephew."

"In that photo? Are you sure? Absolutely sure?"

"Well, he looks clean-cut and overall, more polished now, but I'm pretty sure. I must be wrong because he isn't in the military. I am positive about that. And these men are... gone."

"All but me and one other."

Kaden pulled up a program, and Ivy, still in her towel, watched as Kaden accessed highly classified files and showed her a photo of Fanelli as a clean-cut soldier.

"How about now?"

"Yes, I'm sure."

Kaden began to dig out his files on Fanelli and went deeper to see if he could find anything that might indicate that he was a member of the Marciano Family. Based on his own personal beliefs about the prior teammate, and black ops soldier, he wouldn't put it past him.

After more investigation, Kaden spoke with some energy in his voice. "I need to talk some of this out with you. I can't find a photo of him after the incident that took my team. He had none taken but that one with the team and the military entry photo, but I think I have enough to start putting together a dossier on him. Just in case you're right." And just in case, he had something to finally give credence to his suspicions about Fanelli.

"Kaden, can you tell me what happened?"

"I'll be ready to tell you the whole sordid tale when we're sure you're safe."

Her hand covered his. "Okay. I can wait."

"Thanks, sweetheart. I know it sounds like I'm avoiding what I push you to do. I've come a long way, but still, it's a work in progress."

"Of all people, Kaden, I understand the way things like this can mess you up."

"Right. Now, when was the first time you saw Fanelli?"

"Stephan is how I know him. Well, let me think. It was soon after Marciano and my mom's engagement. I didn't pay that much attention to them then, but I'd say right after going back home. When I left here."

"That fits. Now," a knock at the front door stopped Kaden mid-sentence.

He looked at Ivy, whose eyes were wide and communicated her instant panic. Kaden put his hand up to stop her from speaking. He wished he could have comforted her more than a quick kiss, but there wasn't the time. Kaden was already moving to grab his gun and pocketed bullets. He pushed her out of the office. "It's okay. Get in the bedroom closet."

She hesitated. "Do it. And go into the back exit if I don't come and get you after ten minutes or you think there is danger. And make sure you have your phone to call Jac from inside the exit."

"And grab some clothes. Your naked body is for me alone. But do it quickly."

He checked the cameras. There was an unauthorized woman at the door with bags. Probably why Sharlee didn't call him. He couldn't see anyone else at the door, but he stood, gun drawn and directed at the entrance when the bodyguard spoke through the intercom. "Who is it?"

"Martinique's Boutique. I have an order to deliver to this address. The security guard downstairs said to come up."

Kaden silently nodded at the door, but their guns did not lower.

"No one is home but security. Leave it by the door. I'll be right there."

The lady squealed. "She has her own bodyguard? Cool."

The Gray team member rolled his eyes. "Just leave the bags and take the elevator back down, please."

"Okay. So moody. Do someone a favor, and this is how you get treated. Rich people are all the same."

After the camera and sensors had cleared the floor, the packages were brought in.

"Have her escorted back to her place of business. I think we have someone on the corner. And that front door security guard is fired. Where is our entrance man?"

"Outside in the car. We relied on the front door security to follow the rules and not let anyone up without authority."

"Yeah, he's so fired. I gotta move out of here. Let me go get Ivy while you go over everything in the bag. Do it in my office and call Jac from there. Tell him what happened. And Hampton, shut the door."

The team member didn't change expression. "Roger that."

Kaden holstered his gun and headed for the bedroom. He needed to get a few things straight with his girl, and it was about to get a little loud. After a quick glance and seeing no one, he walked into the bedroom, straight to the closet. No Ivy.

He checked for his key. Still in the box. Where could she be? As he was coming out of the bathroom, he called for her.

"Ivy? Ivy, it's me, and you're safe. From intruders, that is."

Ivy stood up, fully clothed, from behind the bed. Kaden crossed his arms and gave her the "you're in trouble" stare.

"Why do you have that scowl on your face? Is everything okay?"

"Where did I send you?"

"Well, to the closet, and I was in there. I dressed, but I couldn't hear anything. How would I know if things were okay or not? So, I came to lay down behind the bed." She gave him a crooked frown. "But it didn't help. Your doors and walls are thick."

"For safety, which is why I sent you to the closet. For your protection."

"But I already told you why I moved."

Kaden reached back and closed the bedroom door before taking purposeful steps toward Ivy. She turned to face him as he got closer. "Did you send the order here after I said not to do it?"

"No, I sent Sharlee a text. Here, I'll show you."

Kaden didn't move his eyes from Ivy's face. "What is the name of the store that you sent the information to Sharlee called?"

"To Sharlee? Carolyn's Classy Closet."

Kaden looked alarmed. "Then who is Martinique's Boutique?"

"Oh! Sorry, sorry, I ordered that from Jac and Sharlee's yesterday when I knew we were coming here. I told them I'd pick it up."

"Without telling me. And what possessed you to think you would be able to go anywhere, let alone pick up some clothes personally. How did they get this address?"

"It's the one on file from when I lived here. You can't blame me for the shop delivery. I said I'd pick it up."

"Turn around and be quiet."

"What? I will not. You told me to listen, and I couldn't while I was in the closet."

"Turn around, Ivy, now."

"It's not fair. I told you why, damn it, and it isn't my fault they delivered. I thought the security was supposed to stop that from happening. Your security didn't buzz us."

"I'll take care of that right after I take care of one naughty woman who hasn't learned to mind when it is in her own interest to do so."

"I told you I don't mind anyone. That's archaic."

"Well, you might say what we are about to do is equally archaic, but it's happening. Now turn around unless you need me to use my belt."

"What! Oh!" Ivy turned, then began to plead her case. "Please, Kaden. I didn't know."

"Ivy, baby, just shut up. One more word, just one, and I'll take the belt off. Now, pull down your pants, climb on the bed, on your knees, bottom on display."

"Okay, look, I might have psychologically blocked the memory because I just want to live a normal life. I promise I really did forget."

"It could have forced the issue to finish, but Ivy, you could have died."

"Or you. I know. I'm so sorry it happened."

He heard a whine and stifled his smile. She was so damn cute, but this was a serious lesson she needed to commit to memory. Besides, he had yet to spank her for the deceit over the flash drive and the business card. Secrets were her biggest challenge. Time to clear the ledgers.

Chapter Eleven

K aden didn't speak in that firm quiet voice that she had come to expect. This Kaden was keeping things together because of the tight rein he was holding on his emotions. His stiff body and hard tone were different.

"Hampton is still in the other room, and while what you said was true, the walls and doors are thick, some sound still carries. I don't think you want him to know that he is guarding a naughty woman who can't follow orders, so her boyfriend is spanking her ass."

"I'm not an agent, or in the military or an employee for a reason, Kaden."

"And there it is, your mouth just bought five swats with my leather. Want to make it ten?"

"Popsicle."

Kaden finished removing his belt and tossed it beside Ivy on the bed. He sat on the side and pulled her down on his lap. "Ivy?"

"It's just that I don't like to be told what to do. And I don't want to be punished when I don't do what you want. I'm an intelligent woman, and I want respect."

"Baby, listen to me. I respect the hell out of you, but I also can't lose you to some stupid indiscretion. I promise you that no one who is out to harm you will care a whit that you're intelligent, funny, sassy, and the woman I'm totally, completely, head over heels in love with. No one."

"You are?"

"I am, but the Marciano Family must be getting desperate because they have done some bold things to get to you and keep you quiet. I don't think they want you as much as what you have, and possibly to silence you. They're watching this place intently. About every hour, a member of their gang is seen passing the place."

"Why didn't you tell me?"

"I've been a little busy this morning if you've forgotten. You should do what I say out of trust that even if you don't know the whole story, it is enough that I said it was important to do. I discipline, but not because I don't respect you. I do it because I love you and must know you will follow my rules to be safe, no matter what you think about the situation or whether you think you earned it or not. You follow my directions because you trust me. When you don't, I need to impress upon you that your life, mine, and others could be on the line. I have to know you will follow my instructions to the letter so I can concentrate on protecting you. Now. Are you ready?"

"Without the belt?"

"Nope, you get five swats. Are we good? Done talking?"

"I'm doing this under protest."

"Do you agree?"

Her shoulders dropped. "Yes, I agree to the discipline, but I'm not saying I was in the wrong, totally."

"Understood."

"I'm just giving over because I love you too."

He kissed her hard. "Thank you, sweetheart, but the idea is for you to trust me. Now, you know what to do."

As she was scrambling up to get into position, Kaden admired her beauty. His girl had spunk, and he didn't want to break that free spirit, but she needed a little taming. That was his job as her lover and the man who loved her. And he always tried to fulfill his responsibilities. He'd always do what he could to keep her safe, and that happened by her learning the boundaries and staying within them.

He caressed her gently, rubbing her buttocks, her upper thighs, which he was careful not to harm when he disciplined. The first echoing smack was followed by five more, evenly distributed over her whole backside. A blush showed as he continued to pepper her bottom, graduating his swats to land heavier and harder as he continued to impress upon his woman how much he loved her.

Ivy began to wiggle with his spanks, and Kaden looked at her skin, making sure he was still within reason. Red, but nothing else. Good to continue.

"Ivy, I told you to do something, and you didn't do it. Tell me what you intend to do next time."

"Listen, I'll listen when you are trying to protect me. I promise."

"And what about forgetting to tell me about that order. You knew we were so careful with you."

"I guess I just wanted to be my normal self. I didn't think, Kaden. I just didn't think, then I forgot about it. I already told you that."

"And are you going to check with me if there might be a chance I would have something to say about your choices?"

She didn't answer, and he added six more solid smacks to her sit spots. Ivy's wail was partially stifled, but he had no doubt that his point had been made.

"Ivy?"

"Yes, yes," her breath was coming in short gasps. "I'll tell you."

"And now we are to the deception. You didn't trust me, which I understand some of, but you knew we were doing all we could to keep you safe and needed everything you had. You lied to everyone, lied to me, about what you knew and what you had. I won't ever accept a lie. We talked about this, and now I'm going to show you why it is always in your best interest to be honest with me. For us."

Kaden picked up the worn leather. It was his favorite belt. He'd owned it a long time. It was perfect for tenderizing his girl's bottom for lying.

"I'm adding five for lying that could have gotten you killed. The last is for your mouth. Using it for the wrong things and pushing me to follow through on my threat. Remember, I always follow through."

The squeals and grunts were soon joined with kicking calves. She tried to cover her thighs with her feet to impede his delivery and soon discovered that wasn't a good idea when the leather landed on her lower legs.

"Ouch, ouch. Kaden, that hurt."

"Keep them down. These last ones are going to count."

Ivy didn't cry easily, but by the time the belt hit the bed again and Kaden was rubbing her bottom, she sniffled.

"Come here, baby. It's over. Let me hold you."

He helped her pull up her pants and smiled when she hissed. He wasn't hard on her. It was the reason for the swats that she felt more than the actual smacks. He kissed her and laid down next to her on the bed. After a slight hesitation, she cried in his shirt. Nothing sexy about this spanking, and they both knew it.

"I'm sorry. I hardly ever cry."

"I know, but after the time you've had the last year, I think it about time, don't you?"

"Maybe. So, you spanked me to make me cry?"

"Not really. I disciplined, and that often will bring you to tears. This was serious, and I think you know it. Besides, pent up tears aren't good. Take a nap, baby, then we are packing up and going to a safe house. I won't be there as much, but I think the women will be there after I tell the team that we are still being watched and what's on the memory chip."

"What? But I'm comfortable here. It's familiar. I promise I didn't do anything else."

"No, it's not that. I have things to get done, and we have to strategize and work the plan. The place I'm taking you will be safe, and it even has a panic room. I'll let Sharlee tell you about her experience."

"Sounds... interesting."

Ivy's silence was heavy. Kaden waited for her to find her words. He thought she would still be on the spanking that she wasn't happy about allowing, but she didn't seem to be at all concerned about it. She had more on her mind, and it was important to get it out. As much as he wanted to push her to let it out, to trust him with her inner thoughts, he forced himself to wait.

"Kaden, I'm scared. I don't want to be, but I am. I feel like I've been afraid for so long, I don't know how to be anything else."

"Let me take care of keeping you safe."

"I want you to take over and just handle this mess, but I'm still worried that if I let my guard down, even a little, then I'll regret it. Something will happen that will undo everything good that I have or hope to have."

"Honey, I thought you said you were better after the therapy. I'm not saying it isn't expected that you'd be cautious, but this sounds like more than worry. It sounds like anxiety."

"It is. I am much better than before therapy, but being a counselor, I know that head knowledge is not the same as experiencing it. We all have our particular vulnerabilities. I don't want to lose you because you were taking care of me. I'd never get over that loss and guilt."

"I know what I'm doing, and I hear you about the anxiety. It's time you trust me and my abilities, and don't let down your guard. Be careful. Be smart. But also rely on my instincts, abilities, and training. And know that we are so close. It will all be over soon."

Kaden cradled Ivy and heard her inhale hesitantly. He rubbed her back and kissed the top of her head. "There's one thing you need to hear, though. You have to promise me that no matter what I say or one of the guys tells you, no matter how much you don't want to do what you're directed to do, I want you to follow the instructions without a fuss. Do it because you know I can't do my job well if I have any doubt that you aren't where I think you are, doing what I told you to do."

"What if I can't?"

"You can. Do I need to give you a strap to carry around as a reminder that you are to do as you're told when you could be in danger?"

Ivy sat up. "Absolutely not. I don't need a physical reminder of what you can do with a strip of leather, thank you."

Kaden chuckled, and Ivy gave him a little smile. "Then you agree to do as you're told when it's for a good reason?"

"Yes, but you agree there are no more belts?"

"No belts unless you get yourself in deep trouble again over safety and put me in the position of having no choice but to use it.

"That's not fair, Kaden."

He kissed her with tenderness. "But you will accept the terms, yes?" Her crooked frown said she wasn't happy about the terms, but her eyes said she would ultimately give in.

"I suppose."

"Ivy."

"Okay, I accept the terms no lawyer would ever agree to."

He smiled. "That's okay, you aren't one." He kissed her again, another slow and easy one. Ivy sighed contentedly.

From the other room, Hampton called out to Kaden. "Sorry, baby, but it's time to finish this mess. Up you go."

Ivy stood, fully expecting Kaden to leave her in the bedroom to take that nap he mentioned, and that was totally impossible for her to do now, while he went to see what his coworker had to say. As he started for the door, her hand was caught up in his.

"Well, come on. Let's get this done."

"Yes!" she cheered.

She might not know what was necessary to put this whole thing to bed, but she did know Kaden and his team would figure it out. That little bit of confidence in him soothed her many other demons.

THE WHOLE TEAM AND Ivy were on teleconference later that afternoon.

"Shouldn't we do it ourselves?" asked Carter.

"He's right, Jac. The Feds mess things up," agreed Mark.

Jacquard held up his hand for silence. "No, our job, which we did for free because of the assist on our building, was to help them bring down the shipments-*on their own*. We did that by giving them everything they need to do the job. And they have done a surprisingly good job with our security system upgrades. Our part is over, officially."

Ivy piped in hopefully. "Maybe the whole thing is over."

"If that were only true," mumbled Garrett. "So, no safe house?"

"Not today. We always have that as a fallback plan. Right, then we go on with our other jobs and call this one done. I'll keep my hand in just to make sure they do the entire job," promised Jac. "And Charlotte will keep her eye on things."

Kaden wasn't ready to let go because he didn't feel his girl was safe. And he hadn't taken down Fanelli. Not yet. His gut hadn't settled. He would keep a bodyguard on Ivy at all times and keep her home as much as he could while he also kept an eye on Fanelli.

AFTER WEEKS OF BUSINESS as usual and nothing happening, Ivy decided she had had enough of sitting around. It was time for action. Obviously, the Fed's had done what they needed to do, and things were going to be back to normal, well, a new normal anyway.

"Levi, you don't have to be my bodyguard anymore. It's all over. I'm going back to my house to get my things. I miss my stuff."

"Get Kaden's permission."

"Seriously? He's working."

"He's working security. He can answer the phone."

Ivy rolled her eyes. "Fine."

She dialed and got his voicemail. Instead of leaving a distinguishable message, she conversed like he was on the other line.

"Kaden. Levi is going with me to grab my things from the house. Levi won't let me make any extra stops. I will be back before you get home. Promise. Okay, love you." She made a face at Levi. "He had to go."

"He was okay with this?"

"Yes, if you go with me and if we don't make any other stops. I need to be home before him. An hour there and an hour back should give us thirty minutes to gather my things. We'll be back long before Kaden arrives."

Feeling a little bad for her deceit, Ivy kept her conversation and their time quick. She had already made a list of what she wanted to grab, and with Levi watching the perimeter, she was in and out in less than twenty minutes. As they drove off, Ivy heaved a great sigh of relief. She did worry that something might happen, even though it had been nearly a month since Jac had turned over all the information to the Feds.

Once they were out on the main road, nothing more than an overgrown country road between the house and the highway. Four SUVs seemed to materialize out of nowhere. Two pulled out in front of their vehicle. As they passed the place where the two had emerged, another two came in behind them, effectively boxing them in. The occasional car kept them in one lane, for now.

"Call for back up, Ivy. Give them the coordinates from your phone." Levi was already talking to someone. State police. The SUVs tried to force Levi off the road, but he held firm as he tried to get them to the highway and freedom. She got Sharlee and let her pull the information she needed from her phone. Ivy was too rattled to send it. The highway was in sight, about a quarter-mile from them. The SUVs boxed them in tight and slowed down.

Levi tried to circumvent the car directly in front of them, then she heard a gunshot and a quick pop. They careened off the road.

"Did they shoot at you?"

Levi spoke into the car. "Our tire. Hurry, Sharlee. A little shy of gun power here."

"I have called all hands, Ivy. Tell Levi."

"They are sending everyone." Her phone went flying. She hit her head, but not too hard. "Oh God, Levi, I'm so sorry!" She scrambled for her phone.

"Down, get down, Ivy."

Ivy prayed Levi could hold them off, but she knew she had gotten him and herself killed. All for some fucking things. Levi yanked her from the car, dragging her along with him as they ran through the field, but their assailants were right behind them. Then more gunfire. Levi went down, and as Ivy stopped to help him, he threw his body over hers and went totally still. Ivy put her phone in her bra, yanked her pendant off, shoving it in his inner breast pocket and prayed like she did as a little girl. *Help us.*

Chapter Twelve

When Levi came to, in pain and immediately on alert, if only groggy alertness. He assessed his environment and relaxed a little. He was in the hospital. The whiteboard on the wall just to the forward right of him said he'd had abdominal surgery. He couldn't move between the way he was trussed up and his aching body. All that filled his head was that he desperately needed to get to Kaden. He'd been shot, but he was alive. Where was Ivy?

Sharlee walked into the hospital room, grabbing Levi's attention.

"Levi, thank goodness. I wasn't sure if you'd be okay or not. The bullet was in an odd position in your back, but your vest did help stop it from doing any major organ—"

The woman was acting as though she was coming to a social. "Sharlee, they got Ivy." Levi didn't even recognize his own voice. "Marciano's people got Ivy." He tried to convey the urgency of his message.

"We know, remember? She called us? The guys are on their way to find her with all the artillery and personnel they had available."

"Thank God. How long have they been gone? When did you last get an update?" His mind and voice were clearing.

"Um, about an hour ago. I've been trying to monitor things, but they went dark then."

Going dark could mean they were at the target, or it could mean they were in trouble. "And how long has she been gone?"

"Five hours. I'm trying not to obsess, so don't you start. The guys are well trained for this type of operation, having done it countless times." Levi heard the recited mantra. Sharlee wasn't obtuse; she was being optimistic or at least trying to be. They both knew what going black could also signify.

"Jac left us the Orange Team. They are a little bit crazy," her smile was an effort only, "but great bodyguards. I think you know them pretty well. They're your last team, right?"

"Yeah, I know them."

"Good. Becky and Jessie are at the safe house with two team members, two for me and two for you. I think that's a fair division." He could hear her rambling. She needed to get back to her baby, computers, and her security.

He tried to sound stern, but it was a pathetic attempt. "You need to go home, Sharlee."

She sighed, giving him a sympathetic smile. "I know. Actually, I need to go see Storm and wait on the news. I just had to tell you the lay of the land. I never get to have any fun these days." She didn't smile.

"I failed in my mission." There, he'd said it.

"Nope, you didn't. You laid on her to protect her. You covered her with your damn body, Levi."

"How do you know that? I don't even know that. I took my revolver from my inner holster and sat it on the center console. I reached for it, but it was thrown when I needed two hands to keep the car upright. Kaden is going to hand me my ass."

"She left her pendant in your front pocket under your vest as a message that she had been there. Under you."

"Why didn't she run? Was she shot?"

"Honestly, I don't know. We figured she did what she did to tell us what you did for her."

Levi finished her thought. "In case she doesn't get out of this alive."

"In case neither of you did. She probably thinks you're dead since you were passed out by the time the guys got there. Likely you were when she was taken, too."

"They want to shut Ivy up and get what she has. Kaden is going to rip that JJ's throat out. And every motherfucker in that family. I'm missing all the fun." He didn't sound like he was disappointed or joking. His groan alerted Sharlee that he needed his meds. She called the nurse.

"We both are missing the fireworks., You rest and get well. I'm sending your detail in and don't try to get rid of them. Jac promised to cut off their dicks and feed it to them if they left you unprotected, so do them a favor and just let it happen. We'll have a big show and tell party when it's all over. You know, that's how we roll. Take care, and I'll see you tomorrow."

Sharlee left and took two of his former teammates with her, leaving two. His boss knew him too well because all Levi wanted to do was help recover Ivy or join the others watching the women. For their sake, he didn't push the point because he was glad to have them. Levi took a hit of pain meds and went back to sleep.

IVY OPENED HER EYES in a darkened room with one dull yellow light overhead. Not knowing exactly where she was, it took a moment to orient herself to the situation she was in. As she concentrated on the events that brought her to this unfamiliar environment, the memories came crashing into focus.

Levi was dead. He'd tried to protect her. He'd told her to run, but how could she leave him? He saved her life as his body took the bullet and shielded her from it. But she didn't remember anything after that, and her chest hurt. Seems his dead weight bruised her.

Tears raced down her cheeks in the horrific realization that she had gotten Levi killed. Kaden had told her to stay. She could have listened to him, continued cooking like a madwoman to settle her nerves and boredom, but no, she had to get her own equipment, her own things. Jac and his group would never accept her now, not as a part of them. She had killed one of their own.

Kaden would have nothing to do with her, and she didn't even know where she was. The emotional pain was so strong, she knew what others felt when they said they just wanted to lay down and die. But she was stronger than that, or she had been before this. All this from being introduced to one person: James Jester, JJ.

The door opened, and none other than JJ himself swaggered in the room with a sad smile on his face.

"Ivy, I'm so sorry that it has come to this. I wanted to give you everything in exchange for a little obedience, but you didn't accept what I could offer. You went to the security company and to that old boyfriend, Kaden Trainer. Ah, I see you are surprised. I can find out anything. In this case, when you didn't return home, Carlton and I convinced your mother that you were missing. She told us about this man on the outskirts of Lexington. Did you think they could protect you?"

Ivy fixed JJ with a look of such hatred, a lesser man would have cringed.

"I have spies everywhere, and if I don't, I can buy them. It doesn't take much to buy temporary help." He shrugged as though it were of no consequence. "But now the games are over, and I need what you stole from me."

"JJ, I don't steal. What are you missing that you think I took?"

"Ah, you want to play a little cat and mouse, eh?" he nodded his head to the left. "I can play for a few minutes."

The slap delivered rang in her ears and brought tears to her eyes. Her hand went immediately to her cheek. The handprint was already rising. "I changed my mind. I don't have time for games, but I can play this one." Grabbing her hair and yanking, bringing more tears to her eyes, he yelled., "Where is the drive."

Ivy sucked in a deep breath and slowly exhaled, trying to find her inner calm, her inner strength. She had no idea how many people were in the building or how to get out. She could have used a forbidden yet debilitating move against JJ that would have incapacitated him, but it was too risky.

"What are you talking about?" Her confusion was clear.

"That day I threw money from my pocket on the table to pay for your Uber ride. You took more than money."

"I didn't even take your money. If you had counted it, you would have seen I didn't even touch a dime or anything else you tossed on that table. All I wanted was to get away from you and get my car. You hurt me, and I'm not a stupid woman. I left as soon as you turned your back."

He pulled her hair tight again. "Very clever, but you did take something. It was a business card and a flash drive because when I returned, I found it missing."

"And all your money?" She hurt, but she stared him down. It was her only hope of getting him to believe her.

"No, but why would you need money if you had that flash drive?"

"Would you listen to yourself? Why would I even know what was in a drive from your pocket, even if I did see it, which I did not."

JJ looked non-plussed and let go of her hair. Ivy sighed. "JJ, I don't know what happened to your drive, but don't you think that it's possible that someone already there might have taken it? I mean, were you the only one who knew what was in that drive or that it was important?"

"And the business card?" She could hear the hesitation. He was having his doubts now.

"Why would I want your business card? I know how to find you."

After staring at her for a few more moments, JJ abruptly walked from the room. Ivy waited, praying she didn't lose it. She tried to slow her mind, but it was so hard. Just as she was beginning to think they had forgotten her, a man she hadn't seen before came in and roughly pulled her from one room to another.

"Where are you taking me?"

"To wait for the boss."

"JJ?"

He smirked. "Marciano."

She was alone again. The light was not much better than the first as dusk fell. Things were quiet except for an occasional chair that scraped across the floor. She prayed Levi had, by some miracle, survived. And equally importantly, she prayed Kaden would find her before JJ returned with Marciano.

Ivy hoped the guys got to her soon. She wasn't sure how she would fare once Marciano arrived in a few hours. Not well, she imagined. Bad luck that the scuffle had knocked her cell from its securely hidden place in her bra once she got to the holding building.

As crazy as it seemed, Ivy wasn't under lock and key when the group of operatives arrived, just as darkness descended. Kaden and Company already had their plan set up. Night Stalkers were night operators, and while Kaden had enjoyed the thrill of the hunt, this one was personal. He didn't enjoy one second his woman was not under his protection.

Later the guys would say it was anti-climactic, but Kaden liked it that way now that he had Ivy in his life to stay. Being extra good at his job was more important now. Getting his workouts in was never a challenge, but now, he had to focus on the right combination to get what he wanted. While Kaden didn't get to eviscerate anyone, like he desperately wanted to do to relieve his angst, he was relieved Ivy was safe. When they found her, only two men kept guard over her, and the doors were unlocked. Kaden grabbed his girl and held on tight.

She cried but said little as she tried to crawl into his skin with him. He nearly lost his own composure, but Kaden contented himself in having her in his arms and soothing her fears. He held his tongue on asking the appropriate questions. That would come later. For now, they were headed to the safe house, and it was time to end this shit now.

"JJ believes me that I didn't take the flash drive or business card because he just left me there." All Kaden could do was nod. But was Marciano so willing to let her go?

Jac sent Sharlee several messages and then settled in for the ninety-minute drive to the safe house. Ivy, who was only held for six hours at best, was afraid to let go of Kaden. No fear though, he was holding her tightly.

As the men debriefed in the van, Jac contemplated who to contact for the best response and the best deal. They might get paid for this gig yet, which made Jac happy since there was no way they could leave this FUBAR with the Feds any longer. They took too damn long and were too damn lax. Jac ran a tight ship and expected others to do the same.

Sharlee had a cat and mouse game to play with the Feds. That made her happy. Ivy was safe, that made Kaden happy. Ivy was with Kaden, and that made her happy. But the mob wanted what Kaden had: Ivy. It was time to give Marciano bigger game to hunt and, if all went well, make him the prey for once. Jac would get out his big guns.

Chapter Thirteen

Ivy had hoped that coming here to the safe house would not have been necessary, but after her careless move, they had decided to wait another three days: days she, Kaden, Garrett, and Monroe had spent in the sparsely furnished house. The guys were horsing around, strategizing, and playing cards between sports shows, wilderness survival shows, and war movies. Kaden jumped on the PC every so often, and Ivy was reading and cooking and beginning to complain.

Now that she wasn't as frightened, she was irritated she'd lost her phone in the scuffle.

"I feel like I have wasted years of my life just sitting around."

"I still have my rubber paddle to make things interesting," offered Monroe, without looking in her direction.

"Kaden, I need a phone. Look, I'll give you money, and you can go buy me one."

"Ivy, I said you had to wait, and if you offer to pay for everyday things again, I am going to borrow Monroe's paddle."

"Whatever, dinner is ready in fifteen minutes. Just pull it out of the oven and eat. I'm not hungry."

Ivy turned and walked up the stairs to the bedroom. She heard Kaden take the steps two at a time. She kept going to their room and crawled into bed to read. It was her fourth book in three days, and she was a little tired of it too. The bed dipped under his weight, and Ivy looked up.

"It won't be long now."

"And then what?" Ivy could see Kaden had more to say, but he searched for a way to say it.

He reached for her hand. "And then, we'll start our normal."

"I don't think I know what that is anymore."

Kaden took a deep breath and released it. "Ivy, Levi hasn't said anything, but I need to know why you two were out on that road, alone, a few days ago."

She knew he'd circle back to the question eventually. "It was all my fault, is that what you wanted to hear? All me, so if you want to be done with us because of it, say so now. I'll walk out, and you can be done with me."

That grim look overtook his expression again. Disappointment. His fists clenched and unclenched. "Go on."

Ivy couldn't look at Kaden. "I needed my things so I could at least do my graphic business. I mean, it'd been a month. Anyway, I told Levi you said if we went straight there and back and I was home before you were, we could go. Levi thought I was talking to you on the phone, but it was your voicemail."

"That's what I thought when I heard the message that night when it was all over. What the hell were you thinking? No, I don't want to know."

Kaden stopped talking, and Ivy waited. While it was a good technique to get someone talking, Kaden didn't fall for it. He remained silent for a while.

He'd gone silent for much too long. "Are you going to say something?"

Kaden stood. "Nope. You are going to have to work this one out alone." The man walked out the door.

He would have made a good psychologist. Leaving the solution up to the offender after you make them see the foolishness and selfishness of their choices was a good strategy. Way to go, Kaden and now Ivy needed to figure out what she needed to do to fix this. As soon as she figured out how broken things were.

Finally, the teams had what they needed to make their takedown work. Kaden had said precious little to her since the other night's disclosure, and she had steered clear of him whenever possible. She'd not figured things out yet. Kaden was true to his word. He didn't offer one sentence of insight.

The women and baby Storm moved in, and the guys threw their gear in the closets.

"Carter said if things work out, we will only be here for one night. I hope he's right because I'll go crazy if I don't have things to do."

"No kidding," said Ivy.

"Oh, Ivy, I'm sorry. You've been on hold since you got here. I'm sorry I was insensitive. We will be just fine."

Sharlee breezed through, and Jessie, always with a tablet in her hand, waved as she found a corner to work on something that had her full attention.

Becky shook her head as she looked at the windows. "Jac had me looking for ages to find the right treatment for windows that made them difficult to see in or out. I learned a lot about privacy glass, I can tell you."

"And they were expensive. I had to juggle the budget to make them affordable and tax-deductible," added Jessie putting her tablet down, obviously taking a break.

"How long have you worked for Jac?" Ivy asked the two women.

"How long? A few years before Sharlee joined the team," said Becky.

"I started a few months before Sharlee," said Jessie.

"So, do they do this for all their jobs? I mean, make you go to a safehouse and wait until they're done?"

"Well, you were with Kaden a couple of months before you went back home, and he worked while you were here, so I think you know that isn't the case," said Sharlee as she and Storm joined the women, "I was held captive by Carter once, in the panic room downstairs."

Becky grinned. "Yes, that is a story to tell when the guys are working off-site. It is a good one."

Sharlee grumbled. "Not for those being kidnapped. But then the fun really began." She shrugged. "It all worked out."

"Mark threatened to bring me here, especially when I was having trouble with the Chinese assistant to the ambassador, but he never did before today. I didn't think I was going to have to stay, though. I had a few things to say about that."

"So, did he change his mind," asked Ivy, "or are you leaving when he does."

"I'm staying. Once Mark makes up his mind, there is little likelihood of changing it."

"Even Jac changes his mind easier," said Sharlee. "I have to get Finley and Storm settled. Fortunately, I have to work while I'm here. No rest for the wicked, or the tech person, except it works for us this time because you will all see what's going on with the guys while they're gone. Ivy don't forget we need to teach you the Keep Safe program. You snuck out of it before, but you are a captive audience now. It saved Jessie's life, and it could have helped you last week."

"Oh, I'm not sure I'll need anything like that. I can handle things with my martial arts."

"Sure, until someone pulls a gun," said Jessie.

Ivy stared at Sharlee, remembering that was exactly what did happen, but this was supposed to end tonight, so why learn it now?

"I'll think about it."

"Ivy would love for you to teach her the program and see a demonstration. Wouldn't you, honey?"

Kaden's tone was pleasant enough, but his expression brooked no argument as he leaned closer and patted her backside lightly. "Kaden, I just don't see..."

Kaden leaned down close and said in a quietly stern voice, "It is a safety precaution, and you will learn it, or my belt comes off again, and you will still learn it, only with a hot seat to make things more uncomfortable. Time to start trusting me, Ivy. Time to participate in your own safety. You never know when life will throw a curveball."

"Sure, maybe later I could learn it," Ivy told them out loud. Participate in her own safety, was that a jab at her for not following his rules? Well, it left her bleeding.

Kaden whispered, "You just can't help but be sassy, can you? I won't forget."

He kissed her ear and walked back to the living room where the men were going over their strategy one last time.

Practicing was part of their getting ready, and Ivy had heard them downstairs doing just that this week. Kaden called it strategizing. Garrett said it was playing Army.

When Sharlee reappeared, she and the rest of the women took sandwich supplies from the fridge, which made Ivy wonder who stocked the fridge. She noticed the beer and chips on the counter, but the beer remained untouched. Everyone took a soft drink instead. Ivy thought it was because no one wanted to drink anything that would dull their senses. When these men were working, they were serious about the work.

The security was pointed out to the newcomers. Hampton's team would take the lead on protecting the women, and little Storm if his nanny should need the help when the guys were gone.

Sharlee took up her position on the sofa, laptop on her lap and began to send photos to the guys of Ivy's mother's wedding reception. As they reverified each guest, Ivy pointed out the man she knew as Stephan. Glancing up in the immediate silence, she saw Kaden's lip curl and his jaw harden. It was obvious the man she knew as Stephan was the man Kaden knew as Fanelli.

"Trainer, confirm."

"Confirmed. That's Fanelli."

No one pushed the identification further. The guys knew what was behind his strong feelings for former operative Joseph Stephan Fanelli. Ivy didn't, but she knew it had to do with the loss of his military teammates.

"Kaden, are you okay? Will Stephan want to hurt you?"

"I can't get into it right now, but believe me when I tell you, the man is only out for himself. He has no compunction about eliminating anything and anyone in his way. Damn, we didn't teach you how to shoot. I should have listened to Mark. You're good, but you can't beat a bullet."

"Kaden, you're scaring me. I *can* shoot, but I *don't* shoot. I'm just rusty, really rusty, but why should that matter. I don't have a gun, and I won't have to defend myself, right?"

Kaden was quiet for a moment, and then, taking a deep breath, he agreed. "You're right." Dropping a kiss on her cheek, he stepped back, preparing to walk back to the guys continuing to plan the next steps and hopefully end this. Ivy grabbed his arm.

"Not good enough. How much danger are we in? How hot is this situation?"

He stopped and turned around. His eyes were evasive and cool. "I can't tell you for sure, but I think you all should go into the panic room when we leave."

"Really?"

"Yes, but that's why we're here, so you ladies can go underground with the baby and be safe."

"Hampton's team can't keep us safe?" Ivy intended to push the point until she was satisfied with the answers.

"Sure, but if they don't have to worry about you and can just defend the position, it's much easier. If they have to worry about getting you to safety and defend things at the same time, it is more likely something won't go to plan because their attention will be divided."

Ivy nodded. "Okay."

"Yeah?" Kaden gave Ivy a look of uncertainty. Like it had been way too easy to convince her. She deserved that.

She gave him a sad smile. "Kaden, you said I needed to start trusting you. I have not been good at allowing you to do what you do best. So, if you say it would be better if we were in the panic room when you leave, then I will be."

Sharlee walked past them, stopping to hug Ivy quickly before continuing on her way, saying, "We all will."

"Thank you, baby." He took a cleansing breath. "Have you worked out the other little issue you need to fix?"

"Not yet, but I will." Kaden nodded as he pressed his lips against Ivy's hard and fast before he strode out of the room. It was at that moment that she knew. Ivy had no more doubts about who she wanted to spend her life with. Kaden Trainer had wrapped her in a love that didn't smother her, demean her, or take her for granted.

He loved her sassiness, her intelligence, and her independence. Ivy knew he would have liked her compliance a bit more often. She was working on it. Kaden had given her space to be who she thought she wanted to be and that had brought her back to him. Unfortunately, he also spanked, but she was sure that she would be the recipient of only sexy ones as she began to trust his judgment more and follow his lead when it was important.

When Ivy's life hadn't settled down after going home, as she had hoped, and in fact had become an oncoming train wreck, she turned to Kaden without hesitation. She loved him, wanted to be with him every day for the rest of her life. Ivy no longer thought of what she could do or would do but what they would do together. She just needed to get through this mess, and if Kaden wanted her in some super protected room so he could take care of business, even though she didn't want that extra layer of safety, she would do it.

Returning to the bedroom, she grabbed and filled her pack and asked Becky if they needed to take some supplies down to the room. Becky didn't even hesitate to respond.

"Did Kaden say we needed to go there when they left? I hadn't heard."

"He thinks it will take the worry off of keeping us protected and let them all focus on getting the job done."

Becky nodded. "I'll gather the supplies."

Sharlee came up behind them. "You know Kaden loves you."

"I do." Ivy wondered why Sharlee decided to mention it now.

"Don't hurt him." Ahh...

"I would never do that. He's it for me."

"Good. Now let's go figure out our part of this thing. Jessie and Becky will bring more things to eat and drink," said Sharlee. "I consume when I'm working and worried."

Jessie laughed. "Don't we all?"

The women were given the bare bones of the plan on the ground. Sharlee was charged with keeping eyes on the safe house's main floor and, through Jac's and Carter's video cam, the field. This was what she did. The others set about making sure they had extras of what they needed and plenty of baby supplies.

"It's getting dark, so we need to get into place. We need to scrub the place of any trace of civilians," said Mark. He looked over at Ivy, who was new to fieldwork. "So, if anyone comes in such as the police or the bad guys, all they will see is the guys' stuff. Nothing that will lead them to think you were here."

Carter added. "Our main goal is to keep you women out of the line of fire and prying eyes."

Kaden folded Ivy into his arms. "We do the best we can to stay under the radar ourselves. If we do that well, then you won't be part of what we do because we won't be connected."

"Got it."

The guys did their final preps, put on their "war paint," as Carter called it, and the women were sent to the panic room. Ivy could feel her pulse increasing as the huge metal door was opened from the outside hallway leading into the basement. It looked like a regular wall, but it slid back, revealing a sophisticated security panel.

One retina scan and an entry code later, the metal door opened to what Ivy could only imagine the inside of a space station must look like. All stainless-steel machinery and flashing lights greeted them on one side, and on the other side of the room were two sofas, a door, and a refrigerator.

"Impressive, isn't it?" asked Kaden, his lips close to her cheek. "You'll be safe here, and I won't have to worry. We have to go so the ladies will have to give you the tour. You have enough supplies to feed an army for a week. Should last you all until we get back later tonight."

There was laughter, but it was minimal and sounded forced. The tension had skyrocketed when Kaden escorted the women and Storm to the panic room. The realities of what their men were about to do sat heavily on their shoulders. Sharlee could get them out if necessary, and their SUV was underground with them, ready to be driven out under extreme circumstances.

The next safe house was over fifty miles away. No one wanted to think about the team's situation if they had to take that next evasive move. The pressure was high to finish this tonight. Kaden and Ivy had too much to lose if this went belly up. It was understood that on this mission, he was the one that would be the most destructive and the most vulnerable. The weakest link.

Carter was Kaden's assigned buddy for this mission. "I'd like to say I'm a professional, and I don't need any fucking babysitter, but because I'm a professional, I know differently. It is a matter of pride, though, that you assholes picked Goliath here to keep me focused."

The team didn't know exactly what they were walking into but having watched the last drop two days ago, they were surprised that the next one was today. Monroe figured it was a pickup, not a drop-off, but either way, it was their job to get in, make sure it was good and then bring in the Feds. Evidently, the alphabet agencies didn't want to sully their hands if it wasn't real. Simple in and out.

Kaden pulled out an envelope and handed it to Ivy. "What's this?" she asked in a hushed voice.

"My will and power of attorney. Hush now and listen. Sharlee has this on record, but if anything should happen to me, which is unlikely with my King Kong bodyguard, but if it does, I want you to have everything I have except my life insurance, which goes to my parents. I never had anyone to give one to, but now I do. I didn't have time to do more than this, but it will cover. We'll make things more concrete when I get back."

Ivy stood straighter and said in a no-nonsense voice, "You're damn right you'll be back. You do this all the time, Trainer. It's your fucking job to get in, do the deed, and get out. Don't mess this up. I've got plans." She sounded tough, but she just wanted to curl up in his lap and cry like a baby.

Kaden didn't attempt to hide his next remarks delivered with a grin. "I hope one of the first things on your plan is a taste of my leather. My girl does not talk to me like that."

"Come back, and we'll negotiate." Tears were sliding down her cheeks. "Come back to me, Kaden."

"Count on it, my sassy girl."

The men had kissed their women quickly while they were upstairs, and Kaden dropped a grease paint kiss on Ivy's lips before disappearing behind the steel door. The door was closed, the techno beeps of the locks engaging in a room screaming in silence. Sharlee wasted no time getting her surveillance up, and for the next few hours, the women's entertainment was teaching Ivy the Keep Safe program, playing with Storm, and watching the guys watch the target site.

"Okay," said Jessie, "This is how it works. The code is a number, a symbol, and a letter. Simple but difficult to accidentally reproduce. Mine is '1*N' so I can either punch in the code or say, in a perfectly normal sentence, 'one star in' put in a slight pause, and then finish the sentence 'the sky,' or whatever, and the phone will activate, connecting to Kaden and Sharlee."

After several practice runs in which they decided Ivy's activation phrase needed to be changed, they settled on "2@T because, for some reason, Ivy could remember that. She got a chance to learn much more about these women and heard their stories. Sharlee's story of being targeted by one of the people she had worked with as a private pentagon contractor using the code name Vapor was fascinating.

And then the story of Jessie when she got in with some unscrupulous international people just because she wanted to help her brother. Mark had been pretty hot that she had done things on her own.

"Yes, suffice to say, he kept his paddle close at hand for weeks."

Becky clicked her tongue. "Well, you were also part of a federal agency clusterfuck that also involved the mob, the Chinese government double-cross, and her previous accountant job."

"And don't forget the brave woman who gave her life for Jessie's," added Finley from the door of the only bedroom where Storm was napping.

"Now I know why Mark is so protective of you," said Ivy.

"Somedays, it would be fine if he eased up, though. At least he has put away the paddle." The women laughed.

Finley, the Marine turned nanny that seemed to have a hard exterior, laughed as well. The women learned that Finley's name meant fair warrior, and her dad, also a Marine, never let her forget she was a capable woman. Ivy thought that was a pretty important lesson for the dark golden blonde who stood about five feet four inches tall. It led people to underestimate her, and that could be a fatal mistake even now.

"Finley, did you have some code name like the guys did? Kaden said his name was just his last name because of his photographic memory. He was always training people about something. Kaden is evidently great at things like scanning a room and recalling what he saw. I think that is why he is so obsessed with something about Marciano's nephew. He remembers something terrible about him in great detail."

"Yes, he is good at those kinds of things. It's not always a blessing," said Sharlee.

"Too bad, Ivy," said Becky.

"Too bad? Why?"

"Because I rely on Carter, forgetting some of my transgressions. I tend to get so involved in what I do, work, binge-watching a series, cooking new recipes, and so on, he thinks that I need reminding to stay within my limits. But Carter tends to forget sometimes. Kaden won't forget anything."

"Yeah, but I can distract him," said Ivy, wiggling her eyebrows.

Laughter sounded good in the middle of the stressful day, but even that was subdued. "And to answer your question, Ivy, I was called 'Firecracker' because I was quick, mouthy, and could do damage to my opponent."

"Oh. Were you okay with that?"

Finley shrugged. "I've heard worse. It was hard being a woman in the marines. I think it's hard being a woman in the military if you have ambition, but the marines have this macho reputation, and I worked hard to meet that standard. I alienated some and intimidated others. Especially any civilian male."

"Well, you're a civilian now. We need to find you a guy," said Jessie.

It seemed as though Finley was about to tell them something, but instead, she dismissed the idea. "I have my hands full right now. Maybe when Storm gets bigger, I'll try again."

"You're the nanny, not the mommy. Any time you want some extra time off, just shout," offered Sharlee.

"Roger that."

Ivy showed them some martial arts to pass more time, all the while keeping one eye on the monitors for any change. Ivy agreed to give a class for the ladies after things had settled down again.

Sharlee leaned forward and started clicking some keys. "Something is going on."

All eyes were glued to the three screens in front of the computer queen. "We should have made popcorn," said Finley. No one answered.

Jac came over the mic. "It's game time, boys."

The panic room was on mute, and the men had night-vision goggles, so the video showed both discernable figures and, at times, nothing. Then they were running. Flashes of light and the crack of gunfire rang out. The women didn't immediately identify the voice that came over the mic.

"That's Hampton. What did he say?" said Ivy.

"Sharlee, acknowledge. Incoming."

"Copy. Going to second level secure mode."

The room was soundproof, but Finley went into where Storm was sleeping and pulled the door partially closed. She could hear what was going on, but any sound Storm made would not be heard to interrupt the women hearing the transmissions.

The internal and external house cameras were tapped into, and Hampton's team was nowhere to be seen. Noises came through the video outside, but nothing inside. There was no way to tell what kind of danger was lurking outside the door of their hidden sanctuary.

Their attention was now divided between their immediate surroundings, Hampton's team and Jac's team. The tension rose exponentially. Sharlee assigned the three remaining women staring into the videos a different camera and monitor to keep track of while working her magic on identifying the threat. Suddenly, Hampton came into view on Ivy's monitor. He made a call for more assistance and went back out of view.

"Threat neutralized and back up with cleaning supplies en route. Maintain alert level until advised otherwise."

"Roger that," Sharlee replied.

Sharlee leaned back in her chair and rotated her arms. Ivy massaged the tightness out of her shoulder and neck muscles. "Mmm, you are my new best friend," Sharlee murmured.

"Look. There's a hand to hand going on. Who is that?" Becky shook her head. "Well, I see Carter, so—"

Sharlee leaned in closer. "So that must be Kaden. He's pulverizing whoever he has on the ground."

The com went black on that monitor amidst their shocked realization that Carter had allowed Kaden some beat-down time.

Chapter Fourteen

Two hours after the monitor supporting the video on Carter and Kaden had gone black, the threat at the house was gone, the threat level moved back to green, level one, and the women were given the go-ahead to exit the panic room. Ivy was worried about Kaden. Sharlee tried to reassure her that he was fine.

"Don't worry, Ivy, it's usually like this. The difference is that this time you know what went on in real-time. Normally, you have to wait, and when they show up, they show up." The women went to bed as they waited.

The shower was running in the attached bathroom when Ivy woke up. Checking the bed, she was disappointed that it was empty. It was four-thirty, and she needed to pee, but what if it wasn't Kaden in the shower? She was disoriented enough to miss the fact that the bathroom was an en-suite. Well, she really needed to go, so she snuck inside and did her business.

"You naked?"

"What? Kaden? Um, no."

"Too bad, I could have done with shower sex right about now."

Ivy stripped her nightshirt off and stepped into the shower. Kaden turned around to her, and his bruised and battered face and upper body shocked her.

"Kaden, what happened?"

"Ivy, it was great. Worth every bump and bruise, believe me. We have a debrief tomorrow afternoon. I'll tell the story there. Right now, though, I need a little after battle sex from my girl."

"But you're hurt."

"Nah, I've had worse. Now, we're a matched set. Come on, I need a reward and balm for my aches and pains."

Ivy grinned and stepped closer to her man. "Okay, soldier, you asked for it," she warned as she grabbed onto his hard cock.

"Yes, ma'am, I did."

Kaden's lips took hers as she massaged his cock. She took her mouth from his and went down on her knees to place her lips where his need was most desperate. His answering sighs and moans told Ivy she was right where she needed to be, supporting her man.

Later that morning, they left the safe house to be sanitized by a company that Jac employed when necessary. Also, prior military, The Cleaning Crew, was used by only the highest levels of civilian ops. Reynaud and Associates were one of their best clients. It was good to have friends. When the Cleaning Crew was done, there would be no sign of who lived there or what went on there.

When Ivy and Kaden finally dragged in the door, it was without an escort. Oh, they put on the alarms, checked that the cameras were online, but it was the first night they had been alone, completely alone, since the night Ivy had shown up over a month ago. Ivy's bruises had gone from black and blue to a blueish green, compliments of JJ and the car accident.

It had been a long month, and Ivy hadn't made it any easier at times. She had yet to apologize to anyone that he knew of. It had been hectic since the incident, except there were several days she could have at least started apologizing to the guys in the safehouse with her.

Kaden hardened his heart against the overtiredness of his girl. Her adrenalin would finally stop overproducing, and she would need to allow her system to renormalize. Ivy would soon understand that when he said she needed to get permission to go places because of danger, she would learn to listen to him.

"Ivy, go to the bathroom and come back naked."

"What?" Her shocked expression said it all.

"Don't make me repeat myself. Do what I say now. I'm not in the mood."

"Kaden, I..."

Kaden turned Ivy around and leaned her over the dining table. A flurry of fast and hard wallops landed on her upturned butt. They were representative of the disappointment and frustration Kaden felt, all fueled by his abject fear of losing her.

"Do you think you can do what I asked now, or do I strip you myself?"

"Popsicle."

Kaden walked into his office and shut the door.

"Kaden, I'm sorry." No answer.

Ivy could understand that he was upset with her and put his life and those of his friends on the line to keep her safe. It was also a government contract, but not in the same way this was about her. He said she had to fix this herself. So, she grabbed the new phone they had gotten on the way home and set it up. Then when all the numbers had been downloaded from the cloud, she called every single one of Kaden's team, starting with Levi and ending with Jac and Sharlee and apologized for her selfishness and headstrong foolishness.

True to form, each guy had his own way of chewing her out and then accepting her apology. Sharlee said that now the foolishness was over, they could get down to being friends. Jessie welcomed her to the "Lucky Ladies' Club." Ivy knew Mark was a sadist. There was no doubt about it. That made Jessie more like Ivy than either had realized. They both had a bit of the masochist in them.

Becky said to remember to bring a cushion to Jac's house in case Ivy needed it. "I'd learn to put one in your car, so you always have it. These men are sometimes bossy."

Sometimes? Apologies offered and accepted, she knocked on the door of the office again. Still no answer.

She could wait him out. Ivy called for groceries to be delivered and put in another order of clothes. This time she ordered sexy lingerie to entice the man she was going to stick with forever. Then she put a load of laundry in and started an early dinner. She would need sustenance and an early night so she could prep all of that now.

Dinner was made, and clothes were in the dryer, so Ivy went to the bathroom and while there, she stripped. It was now or never. She knocked again, more insistently this time.

"Dinner is ready, Kaden. Please come out. It's lonely out here." No movement. "And I'm getting cold." That did it. His protective side would not ignore her. She heard him turn the handle, and she retreated to the kitchen.

Kaden watched the love of his life walk toward the kitchen in her sexy slow gait. For the first time since he had laid eyes on his beautiful woman, he hadn't been aroused by her swaying ass or her pleas for mercy earlier, but now, it was a different story.

He loved her so much he couldn't shake the anger at the agony he went through trying to get to her. Once he found out it was because she disobeyed him, no, ignored him, he couldn't let the agony go. Kaden had seen all kinds of mutilation to women. Those ran through his mind then; only his mind showed Ivy as the one left dead.

Kaden scrubbed his face with both hands and walked over to the bar area. He poured himself some juice. He poured another glass and set it on the bedroom dresser and waited for her. Placing it any closer would jeopardize its survival. Ivy tended to be vocal and physical when he laid his leather on her ass. Today he was going to leather her well. If he had to do it daily to break her of the habit of lying and sneaking and hiding things, he would. If he had to do it twice a day to keep her obedient when it was for her safety, he would.

Ivy walked into the bedroom completely naked. She was beautiful. He had to restrain himself from reaching out and caressing her cheek. Instead, he fingered her hair.

"I'm disappointed in you, baby."

Silence.

"You lied, you sneaked, you endangered yourself and Levi. You disobeyed me when I told you to stay home unless I agreed you could go somewhere."

Ivy nodded. "I know. All I can say is that it had been weeks. I couldn't spend my whole life stuck in this condo. That isn't a life. I wish you would have paid attention to me when I said I needed to get out."

His frown deepened. "Is this where you want to go with me right now? Okay, then you went out and almost got Levi killed. You nearly got yourself killed. We had to step in and risk two teams' lives, Storm's life, and the lives of the women you claim are your friends. So, I ask again, do you want to go there right now?"

"No, you're right. I don't want to shift the blame, just explain what I was thinking at the time. It was selfish and foolish to have done what I did. I'm sorry for putting everyone at risk. I just... it's what I do. I see the prize not the road to get to it."

Kaden was glad to hear her leave off the old mantra that involved leaving. They were getting somewhere.

"Good, get into position and hold on tight. We will start with my hand, move to the leather, and end with the paddle. After I put in your plug. Do you want to safeword out?"

"No."

"You sure?"

"Yes, I'm sure."

"I had hoped you didn't because it at least shows that you understand this was well and truly earned."

Kaden pointed to the bed. Ivy slowly got into position.

"Spread 'em."

Ivy placed her hands behind her and exposed her dark entrance. "Cold." Was all the warning he gave her. He coated his fingers to pave the way. Before he did more than a few strokes of his fingers, Kaden slid the plug inside and seated it well. He patted her butt firmly.

"Now I have a target. Relax if you can, Ivy,"

No more words, no rubbing of her still slightly warm bottom, Kaden commenced. Firm, strong palms landed on her upturned ass. The cheeks were firm from her flexing and tightening.

"You'll bruise and hurt more if you don't relax."

On and on, he spanked, making sure to cover every inch of the spankable zone. Then the sound of a jingling belt buckle and the swish of the leather flying through the loops sent a chill up her spine. He gave her no warning. It wasn't the well-worn belt he had the last time but a work belt. Newer, less pliable. More painful.

Kaden took the type of belt into consideration when he applied it to her red backside, but the surprised squeal was the first of many yips and wails before he had finished his task. Long uniform lines colored her bottom and upper thighs. He was always careful of her thighs, but she needed a little there to feel his meaning fully.

He tossed the black belt to the bed and opened the drawer. Ivy's ass was showing some light purpling where the edge of the belt struck her tenderized skin. He played with her plug for a minute. Drawing the paddle from its place, he changed positions and bounced the leather-wrapped wooden paddle off her nates.

Over and over, he heard the splat when it landed on her butt until Ivy finally broke. Tears that told of her devastated heart gave Kaden relief. He could finish the lesson now. Kaden waited until her tears had slowed down.

"Ivy, I love you. If you cannot understand that you put me through small deaths every time you break our agreements and put yourself in harm's way, then expect to be here again, soon, and often. Each time, the penalty will be a little harder and a little longer. I am determined you will do as I say when it's important."

"I'm trying."

"I know, baby, but this is something you have to get a handle on."

Three more swats and he replaced the paddle. Kaden removed her plug and sat it on the paper towel he had placed on the side table. Then he removed his own clothes slowly and deliberately, taking his time to fold each piece. He left for the bathroom and returned with a warm washcloth to wipe her anal area and allowed the heat to soothe her, then allowed it to grow cold to help her backside.

Finally, when Ivy was down to sniffles and hiccups, he brought her up from her position. The kiss he gave her was warm, gentle, healing. Kaden wanted to give her sweet love, but she wasn't ready, and he didn't want to confuse the lesson. But he could be nurturing. He loved this woman with all his being. Now he would show her how much she meant to him, using sensuality.

Ivy whimpered when Kaden brought her down to the bed. Ivy felt some residual resentment because her wings of complete independence had been clipped, but she'd get over it. A shiver quaked her body as he kissed her gently. Starting from the nape of her neck, down her back and to her well-disciplined bottom, he kissed every spot he passed.

Kaden continued to kiss her welts that still throbbed, his handprints that she could feel the ache of each finger outline, and her paddle outlines with their own particular rings of fire. He tongued her anus and nudged her thighs apart, kissing each inch of exposed skin. Ivy moaned and shivered.

"You are mine, Ivy Linton, and I cannot live without you. Please don't make me."

"Kaden?" came her watery question. "You don't hate me?"

His quiet chuckle sounded good after the swats of his discipline and the tears of her remorse and pain. "Never have I ever, nor will I ever, hate you. I was angry, yes. I was disappointed and hurt, yes, but hate? Not even a second."

Kaden continued to kiss and caress, but he didn't stop to give her an orgasm. She understood. He was making a point but didn't want her to believe he harbored any lingering irritation. He loved her, and she ached for his touch to complete her. Maybe later. For now, this slow sensuality was the sexiest thing she had ever experienced.

When she woke up, it took a moment to understand that the sun was down, and the room was dark because it was night. Her bottom hurt something fierce. Her hand made contact with a warm body that aroused the moment she touched him.

As they lay in bed, Ivy snuggled up close to Kaden, who had donned lounge pants. He said, "You okay, sweetheart?"

"Mmm, I'm good. I'm hungry, and I bet dinner is ruined. Can we order in? I'll pay for it."

"We can order in, but you paying for it? Isn't your ass still throbbing?" Ivy laughed at his look of incredulity.

"Yes, okay, my bad. Can I at least order?"

"You can order. I hate calling in orders."

"Good. I want Italian."

"Carbs, you need them. I'll do a little more PT tomorrow."

LATER THE NEXT AFTERNOON, as Ivy and Kaden arrived at Jac's house, the situation room, soon to be Jac's den again, was full of Kaden's team and the Gray team. When everyone was settled into a spot of the now crowded room, Jac stood and flipped over a whiteboard. There were several items on the list to be discussed.

"Okay, ladies and gentlemen, listen up. The first order of business is our last mission. Ivy, there's room next to Kaden."

"I'm fine. I'll sit in a minute."

"Ivy, dear, it's distracting. Sit next to Kaden."

It wasn't a request, and it was at that moment, Ivy knew that the entire room knew why she preferred to stand and why Jac preferred her to sit. Ivy crossed her arms. Kaden reached over and grabbed her hand. She resisted until he raised his eyebrow. No, she didn't dare risk his ire again. Two spankings in one day were quite enough. Kaden had been zealous about his determination to make her do as he said, when he said, for safety. She was determined to learn quickly.

"Thank you. Now, Hampton, fill us in on what happened on your end."

Ivy heard Jac's words clear and strong, delivered by a man who knew when to focus on business. He was confident and in control of the room. Jacquard Reynaud knew what he was doing, and he did it well. And he sounded like a drill sergeant. Kaden had said Jac was a pretty high officer with a very intense job by the time he decided to retire. The particulars that Kaden told her were lost in her lack of understanding about the military. She was sure that would change pretty soon.

Hampton stood, and Jac sat. "Yes, sir. Two nights ago, at approximately 2330, the Gray team encountered a group of seven males with assorted tools of destruction. They arrived in a black van with darkened windows. We observed them for approximately ten minutes before they exited the van. Once on the ground, they began swinging pipes and baseball bats. Guns were not in view. Once a gun appeared, we decided to settle the crowd with a little pepper spray. We then borrowed their tools to impress upon them that their idea was fundamentally flawed. One shot was fired by the perps."

Mark asked Hampton, "What made you think they were coming after the safe house?"

"Because they didn't attempt to stop anywhere but the safe house. They knew someone was in that house that they wanted."

"How do you think they tracked her?" Jac asked.

"I would recommend checking her clothes."

"The ones dropped off by my shopper and that I brought to her when I got there?" asked Sharlee.

"Don't know, but she was there days before the attack, so I can't believe they were on the clothes that were brought from the house. They wouldn't have gotten the signal after Ivy went into the panic room, so my guess is that there was some device we didn't see."

Ivy spoke up. "But I stripped what I had on before we got there and only brought what we got from Sharlee, clothes-wise. The rest you all screened the first day I got here."

Kaden asked Ivy, "How about your bag?"

"A new one I ordered from the shop that Sharlee had delivered to me. I wanted to make sure I started fresh."

"Charlotte?" prompted Jac.

"My shopper is the only other one besides the people at the shop. She dropped off the groceries too, the day of the operation."

Jac stared at his wife with an expectant expression. Sharlee sighed. "I know, sack the shopper. Man, she was the best one I'd had so far. But how could they have gotten to her?"

Garrett answered. "The likely scenario was this: When Marciano and JJ found her dropping off purchases last Friday after it was discovered that Ivy was here, they targeted her for later use. A few days ago, they used her."

Ivy spoke up. "JJ told me, basically, that if he didn't have a person in the right place, he hired or bought them."

Kaden nodded. "Security guards were bought at my condo building and likely at the office building too."

"Okay, that settles things then. Hampton, can you get your team to go hang out at the safe house about an hour a day for the next week? I want Marciano's people to think you guys live there." Jac turned to Kaden and Ivy. "Get your new things scanned, Ivy. Trainer, dispose of the trackers in the dump."

Monroe spoke up. "It might be a good idea to have our landscaper mow weekly, possibly get someone to show up to be seen every week. I can make a roster."

"Yep, sounds good. Get with Charlotte so only those not doing something else can go. It might be better to just assign teams. We'd have the better success that way, I think." Jac turned to address Hampton again. "Thanks, Team Gray. Good job, guys. I know you have another job waiting on you, so you're free to go." Gray team stood to leave with good-natured teasing following them as they sauntered out.

As he passed Ivy, Hampton bent down and said, "Pleasure working with you, ma'am, but Kaden should have wielded that belt a little longer. You definitely need a little taming."

Ivy laughed and shook her head. These people were born with no filter and less couth. She could learn to live with that because they were good people and loyal to the core.

"Okay, people, who's next? Mark? What happened on your end that night?"

"Everything went as planned. Sharlee's deciphering was spot on. Kaden and Ivy were correct in their identifications of the last unknowns. We waited, went in, eliminated the resistance and captured all the ones we wanted to with no casualties despite Kaden's over-zealous assistance."

"Monroe, what were they transporting?"

"Receiving this time, and it was heroin locked in the bottom of sealed canisters of chips. They will put that shit anywhere."

"Charlotte, did you share your information with the Feds?"

"Yesterday."

"Great. That's done. The Marciano family is down Bubba, JJ, his son Carlos, his nephew James *Stephan* Fanelli, and many grunt laborers. Now, as I see it, this was a large shipment drop. They had a few women and a few guns delivered, which is why all three upper-level people showed up. I figure they each have a branch of shit they peddle."

"Yes," agreed Sharlee, "The Feds intercepted a shipment of arms, except Fanelli wasn't in the group. Before the bust, they heard his name as soon to arrive, but he must have gotten a whiff of trouble because he didn't show. This time he was there."

Kaden nodded. "So, let's just finish the Fanelli issue, shall we?"

"By all means," agreed Jac. "What did happen?"

"I locked on the two targets in the side room from the cargo. I chose Fanelli to take down, Carter took the other fleabag. Fanelli didn't recognize me due to the expert application of war paint." Boos and rude comments followed Kaden's description.

Jac whistled. "Go on."

"Right, well, in the hand-to-hand skirmish that we engaged, it took a little longer than typical to subdue the target, but it was done. Carter escorted Fanelli out of the building."

Jac shook his head. "Right, but what happened to the cam feed? You were to keep that on at all times, so there was no doubt that things went according to the Fed's guidelines."

Kaden shrugged. "It got a little rowdy there for a minute. My camera must have been skewed."

Carter nodded. "We were fine, and my buddy followed procedure. He didn't shoot the guy, so everything else was within reason to subdue a target. You know we try never to use deadly force."

Jac ran his fingers through his hair and stood to get more coffee. "The Feds think you cut the feed because you didn't want your actions recorded. They also said, after you spoke to them yesterday about the connection you had with Fanelli, they appreciated you didn't get them into other shit by showing the beat-down. They are bringing him up on additional charges."

"I'd like to tell you about me and Fanelli and what the Feds now know. I think it will explain enough that you don't think me an asshole for no good reason."

Chapter Fifteen

The room became completely quiet. Kaden looked down at Ivy. "I think you all know that my unit was the 160th SOAR unit. Ivy, you might have heard of Night Stalkers. Specializing in air nighttime missions. That's how I got to Kentucky, through Ft. Campbell. Anyway, my team was solid, well established, but we'd lost a man on a previous mission. The next couple of months were harder, but we were fine because of the low level of difficulty due to our loss. Soon, however, we had an involved mission that needed a full team. We were assigned Fanelli."

"On paper, he looked good. He had a good history, good credentials and his CV was done well. But he was a newbie to us. It took a little extra time to train him to our way of life."

"CV?" asked Ivy.

"His resume." Ivy nodded and leaned back to listen again.

"He got along with everyone, and his skills met our needs, so there didn't seem to be anything else to do but welcome him on the team."

Murmurs came from the team of similar experiences of "looked good on paper," transfers that didn't work out. Kaden continued.

"The mission we had planned for weeks to get right was here, and we took off for parts unknown. It ended up being

Venezuela, but we knew the plan. We executed it flawlessly. Back to the little village about five hours before extraction, the villagers offered to have us eat with them. I was the last to head to the hut because of the final checks and one last perimeter sweep. As I was heading toward the hut, Fanelli was inching his way out of the hut. Sneaking, you know? I asked him where he was going. I said he should eat, and he said he had something to get from his ruck. I told him I'd secured our gear, but he said it was fine. A few seconds later, the place blew. I sustained a fucked-up elbow, but the rest of the people inside were blown all to hell."

"What about Fanelli?" asked Ivy in a near-whisper.

"Nothing. Not a damn scratch. I couldn't figure it out, but I knew something was up. I gave my report. It was the same as Fanelli's. We were extracted on time; only four of us weren't upright. I put in my request to rotate out after my elbow was made bionic, and as luck would have it, Jac was recruiting."

"So, if there wasn't any proof of culpability, why did you pursue Fanelli?"

"Pain and my gut. Seems it was right. Feds tell me that right after the team was deactivated, there were deliveries of guns to Indiana. I guess that is where Fanelli is from as well, so being part of the Marciano family, a branch off Indianapolis' larger mob makes perfect sense."

Carter nodded. "That is why he is the guns guy for Marciano. It's his specialty."

Jac jumped in. "It seems that Fanelli and his connections have further connections in Venezuela and Colombia. South America also exports young people. They have a pipeline, and they were milking it, but that income stream has been broken for all intents and purposes. Feds went backward, found the point of origin and have that staked out for the next shipment they expect to be soon."

Levi moved over gingerly when Finley walked in. She sat stiffly next to him and listened to the ending of the explanations. Jac nodded in her direction as though agreeing to her being in the room.

"Fanelli is being investigated," added Sharlee, "and then they will prosecute according to his charges that are highly likely to include some military sanctions."

"Unfortunately, they won't be able to prove that he set the bomb, but he did have a motive," said Kaden. "It appears that he had military ammo sites and other important information that Camden, our leader, had discovered. Unbeknownst to Fanelli, Camden had sent off an email to command and to the IG, but obviously before the bombing."

Ivy sat up. "What's IG?"

"Inspector General. They look into things that aren't right in all sorts of areas pertaining to the military."

Kaden finished. "So, they have more information. It seems Camden was very thorough in his sharing of information. Thank God for satellites."

Carter jumped in. "So, JJ was in charge of getting women to men who would pay for them. Sound familiar, Miss Linton?"

"Look, I said he gave me the creeps, and I tried to get away from him."

Carter smiled. "I know. I just want to impress upon our women that even when we think something is safe, it may not be. That is another reason why the Keep Safe Program should be used if needed."

"I'm still okay with implants." The women groaned. "Just saying." Mark ducked when Jessie hit him with a sofa pillow.

Sharlee wanted to wrap things up. "Okay, so JJ was the people mover, Fanelli, the gun runner, and Carlos was into drugs. With the loss of those men and the loss of another handful of guys due to ineptitude, I worry that Ivy's mother isn't safe. So, I sent the Feds to your mother's place, saying Marciano was living there with his wife and that she knew so much more than she let on. That would put the Feds in their pathway and possibly keep her safe."

"Well, it might help. I can give my mother a call and check on her."

"I prefer that you let them do their thing first. If you call her, do it with Kaden or Charlotte on the line," said Jac. "It's for your own protection."

"Okay. I have to go and talk to the Feds tomorrow anyway. I'll take an overnight bag."

"I would. And a pillow," said Jac. "Hard chairs. Now, is it time for whiskey?"

As the traditional paper cups were passed around with a good whiskey, Jessie declined. "Are you not feeling well?" asked Mark.

"I'm feeling fine. The doctor advised against alcohol for a while."

"Why? What's wrong?" Mark's concern was strong.

Sharlee passed the whiskey tray to Levi. "Nothing's wrong, you idiot. Your wife is pregnant." Sharlee squealed and hugged Jessie.

"What? No. I thought we were going to wait."

Jessie's face dropped all its joyful expressions. "Mark?"

He scrubbed his face and smiled. "I'll be alright. I just thought we'd kinda share Storm a while longer." Mark dropped a tender kiss on Jessie's lips. "I'm very happy we are going to be parents. But I'll have to update security. And you'll need a schedule to follow." Jessie just rolled her eyes.

"And no spankings." Jessie shrugged.

"Okay, we have to think this through."

The laughter finally died down, and talk moved to the new office building.

Epilogue

Ivy walked into the condo and flopped into the chair. "I just sold the lake house."

"Ivy, honey, are you sure it's what you want to do?"

Ivy smiled. "Kaden, we have gone over this. It was my dad's lake house, and he loved to bring his friends and family. My family has changed, and I want something for us. Dad would be happy that I'm happy. And before you ask, you know I am crazy happy."

"Okay, then I have some listings that I think will work for both of us. The one I like the best is a lot of house, but a good deal."

"Let me look."

After examining the realtor pages, Ivy said, "Oh, let's look at this one online." After reviewing the photos and doing some research, they decided to look at several. "I'll check these others out, but I think I already love this one."

"I was hoping you would. I have an appointment for a showing in two hours."

Twenty-four hours later, after one more walkthrough and some research that Sharlee helped them with, they put in an offer for the full asking price.

"And you still want the house for cash?" the realtor asked.

Kaden leveled a look at his girl. "Ivy?"

"Yes, for cash," She said, staring at Kaden, almost daring him to contradict her.

"Great. I'll just go and run the numbers and get the seller's agent on the line to see what we need to do to get you in as soon as possible. I'll be back in a few."

The door closed quietly, and Kaden looked at Ivy sternly. "You are using the money from the lake house, and that is your money."

"Yes, and now it's our money paying for our house. Kaden, I want to do it. It will save us so much in fees and interest."

"It's a good idea, but we should split the costs."

"Why? I'm using our money."

"Your money."

"I had it deposited into our joint account. Oh, and while we are at it, I'm going to a huge home show in Georgia. Want to come?"

"What? Who's going with you?"

"Just me if you can't go."

"It's not safe to go alone. Look, it's about safety, so you are going to listen to me. I don't want to take your independence, but I refuse to let you run wild."

"Wild?" she responded in a subdued whisper. "I'm not the one who turns their video off, so no one knows what I do in the dark."

"I took care of business. No one died. But I do believe that neither Jester nor Fanelli will be able to get out of this mess. And you, my girl, won't either. Do you speak to me in that tone?"

"Not usually."

"The answer is no, sir or no, Kaden. We will address this when we get home."

"Good, because I haven't had a good time between the sheets in a couple of days, and I'm getting a little desperate."

Kaden contemplated Ivy. "You did that on purpose."

"Yep. Worked."

"Oh, it worked alright. I have a new strap..."

Ivy shivered as the door reopened, heat rising into her face. Tonight was going to be fun.

AT THE FRIDAY DEBRIEFING with just the team, Kaden brought pictures and announced they had bought a house.

"It has four bedrooms, a separate studio for Ivy's lessons and an indoor/outdoor pool because it was something Ivy wanted badly. Thanks, Jac." Everyone laughed. "Two offices because I refuse to share. Ivy needs to concentrate on her things, not my work. And a three-horse stable on ten acres."

Jac slapped his shoulder. "I have a feeling she will be looking to fill it before too long."

"Well, so long as Mark is the only father to be for a while, that's fine with me. I need to get used to being a homeowner and a husband before I father any children. Besides, I'm still taming my girl."

Mark groaned. "Don't remind me. Jessie is already cranky and pushing my buttons. There isn't much I can do about it, and she knows it."

Jac grinned. "I've got some ideas for you, Mark. They worked for me." He turned back to Kaden. "And what's this about being a husband? Are you two tying the knot?"

"Oh, didn't I tell you? Next month. We will move into the house and have a wedding. Ivy has invitations."

Carter groaned. "Becky wants kids but is not ready to get married. I'm ready to get married, but not ready for kids. So, we are waiting for everything."

Garrett cleared his throat. "Word of advice. Get her up the aisle as soon as you can without pushing her. If you don't, the world has a way of getting in the way. You might regret it for the rest of your life."

"Thanks, man." The team knew Garrett's opinion came from a broken relationship he had thought would last.

"Levi, did I hear you and Finley went out to grab some grub this week?" asked Jac.

"Yeah. Talked about life in the marines and out of them. She's funny and smart. Good company, but that's all. We're friends."

"Yep, heard that one before," said Jac. "Remember, she is my kick-ass nanny. I will be sending you on every dirty assignment there is if she leaves before Storm is old enough."

"Monroe, how're the munches going?"

"Yeah, not well. I did meet a cute little thing. She's only a few years younger than me and curious. She'd gone to a few of these meetups, and we made a date for last weekend's munch, but she didn't come. I called the number she gave me, and it went to an automated voicemail. Guess it was more me than her."

"What's her name?" asked Sharlee.

"Mallory S. The attendant looked at her paperwork and said her name was perfect. Even asked if she had picked it for a pseudonym. She hadn't."

"Let me look to see what I can find. The perfect name for a play date."

The End

About the Author

USA Today and Amazon #1 Bestselling Author of historic and contemporary realistic romances with a touch of suspense. Alyssa Bailey, is a dyed in the wool Texan living amongst the beauty of Southeast Alaska who enjoys taking from her own experiences to create fictitious worlds sure to tease the readers palette and invite them to sink into exciting adventures.

Alyssa enjoys writing power exchanges between strong, intelligent, sassy women who are not afraid to make a stand and loving men confident enough to give his woman space, but Alpha enough to keep her safe despite her choices. There is *always* a happily ever after.

Her characters live amongst historical lords and ladies, in the contemporary realm amongst men and women of the world sometimes with a touch of the paranormal or suspense and of course, hard-working cowboys and fiercely romantic American Indians.

Visit me online and sign up for my Newsletter:
http://alyssabailey.com[1]

Join my Facebook Group for fun and prizes:

---

1. http://alyssabailey.com/

https://www.facebook.com/alyssabailey.romance

OTHER ROMANCE BOOKS by Alyssa Bailey

Lords and Little Ladies: Georgian Historical, spicy

Lord Thayer's Choice

Lord Ashton's Decision

The Black Laird Requires

Lord Kendrick's Obligation

The Devil Duke's Distraction (2021)

Chase Abbey Series: Regency, Spicy, Suspense

Lord Barrington's Minx

Becoming Lady Barrington

Lady Caroline's Defiance

His Improper Lady

Safe and Secure Series: Contemporary, suspense, spicy

Saving Sharlee

Saving Jessie

Saving Ivy

The O'Connor Series: Contemporary, Rancher, Saga, Spicy

Liam & Jocelyn's Story-

Her Sweet Complication

Liam's Lessons

Loving Liam

Ciarán and Katherine's Story

His Gentle Persuasion

Rancher's Creed

Katie Consents

Quinlan and Cheyenne's Story

Quinlan's Quest

Accepting His Way

Her Balancing Act

Kelli and Parker's Story
Meeting Her Needs
Kissing Kelli
Keeping Kelli
Cián and Molly's Story
In Pursuit of Molly
Freeing Molly
Forever Molly
Clearwater Ranch -Contemporary, Spicy
Piper's Plan
Camille's Second Chance
Josie's Refuge
Lone Wind Series: Contemporary, spicy Native American
Reclaiming Clover
Taming Texanna -American Historical, Native American, Spicy
Cowboy Welcome- Contemporary, Spicy
In the Spirit of Christmas -Contemporary, sweet
Guardians of Refuge (Contemporary Military Spicy)
SEAL of Refuge
The Strategy of Love
Judging Refuge (2021)
Anthologies (Heat Varies)
Sweet Town Love
Historical Heroes
Hero to Obey
Cowboy for a Cause
Multi-Author Box Sets (Heat Level Various)
Love, Christmas 2 Movies You Love

Love, Christmas 2 Recipes
FREE Book Bites 11
Christmas Shorts
Irresistible Heroes
Tempting Protectors
Sexy and Seductive
Sweet and Sassy Summertime Vol. 2
Dear Santa: A Christmas Wish
Cowboys for a Cause (Limited)
Hero Undercover (Limited)

Don't miss out!

Visit the website below and you can sign up to receive emails whenever Alyssa Bailey publishes a new book. There's no charge and no obligation.

https://books2read.com/r/B-A-MXIL-PCAMB

BOOKS 2 READ

Connecting independent readers to independent writers.

Did you love *Saving Ivy*? Then you should read *Saving Mallory* by Alyssa Bailey!

New town. New Job. One new friend who didn't know her name or address. Would anyone ever notice that a madman took her?

Mallory Sasse was lonely and needed a change. She left her hometown to find a new future and maybe a new lover. Determined to make this change successful, she leased a great townhouse and started her new job as the lead pharmacist, then looked for some fun. At a meet and greet in a nearby town, she met him.

He was fit, authoritative, with a gentle smile and greying at his temples. Monroe took her breath away.

Her attraction grew over the weeks, fast approaching that relationship commitment line. The day she would take that ultimate step, Mallory found herself in the grip of a madman and all hope for a future seemed lost. But after seeing a dying woman in the cellar with her and realizing her destiny if she quit, survival became Mallory's only option.

Monroe Merton was missing something in his life. Retired Army. Great job. Staring at 45 with no prospects of love ahead. He had been okay with that, but as he watched his friends find love, he wondered. Then he met Mallory. After several meet ups in a group, and hours of phone conversations, Monroe knew he was falling hard for her. When Mallory was as ready as he was to take the next step, he asked her on a date. Alone. Hopefully all night. Mallory sounded excited the night before, but when the time came, she never showed. The woman ghosted him. She didn't even answer his calls. She had disappeared.

Just when Monroe knew Mallory was in trouble and he was on her trail, the police call. *"Monroe Merton?"*

Read more at alyssabailey.com.

Also by Alyssa Bailey

Lone Wind
Reclaiming Clover

Safe and Secure
Saving Sharlee
Saving Ivy

Watch for more at alyssabailey.com.